The Horror Of It All

The Horror Of It All Stories

Laughton J. Collins, Jr.

Contents

The Horror Of It All

The Midnight Palace wasn't just a theater; it was the town's dark, beating heart. Its grand marquee, perpetually advertising nightmares like "Flesh Harvest" or "Screaming Walls," pulsed with sickly neon. Crowds gathered nightly, drawn by the chill, the shared screams, the safe thrill. Only horror played here. It was tradition. It was home. People vanished sometimes too. Sam Rigby went in for the midnight showing of "Crawler Cove" and never clocked in at the garage the next day. Old Mrs. Hanson disappeared after a double feature. Most folks just shrugged. "Ran off," they'd say. "Trouble follows some." They ignored the whispers about cold spots in the balcony where breath fogged even in summer, or fleeting, impossible shapes seen writhing *within* the projector's beam itself. They ignored the faint, rhythmic scratching sometimes heard behind the plaster walls during the quietest scenes.

Then came the premiere of "Curse of the Shadow People." The Palace was filled with eager bodies. The air thickened with popcorn grease and nervous sweat. Halfway through, the screen flickered violently. Not like a film glitch. It *rippled*. The shadows *within* the film seemed to deepen unnaturally, to swell beyond their frames. The image tore. The heavy screen fabric shredded like fragile parchment, top to bottom. Darkness poured out. Not just darkness – shapes. Tall, impossibly thin figures with elongated limbs and featureless shadowed faces flowed onto the stage. They moved with silent, liquid grace, absorbing the light around them.

The audience froze. This wasn't part of the show. A nervous laugh died instantly. Silence stretched, tight and suffocating. Then the exit doors at the front burst open. Not from the lobby outside. From the auditorium aisles themselves, as if the air solidified and ruptured. More things emerged. From the screen tear and the darkest corners of the theater, peeling themselves out of the velvet drapes and the sticky floor grime. A hulking figure in a grease-stained mechanic's jumpsuit and a crude, welded metal mask, dragging a heavy, blood-rusted pipe. Something sleek and unmistakably, insectoid, its segmented body dripping thick, iridescent fluid that sizzled on the carpet. Pale children with eyes like lumps of coal, fingers ending in needle-sharp points. A man whose face seemed crudely stitched together from mismatched patches of decaying skin, threads pulling tight over a crooked grin. They weren't actors. They smelled of decay, spoiled meat, and raw, ancient malice.

1

Screams erupted, genuine and deafening. Panic tore through the crowd. People scrambled over seats, clawing at each other, trampling the fallen in their rush towards the exits. The slasher swung his pipe in a wide, brutal arc. Wet, crunching thuds silenced shrieks mid-breath. The insectoid creature reared back, its mandibles clicking, and spewed a stream of acidic fluid. It hit a fleeing man in the back; his scream cut off as his flesh dissolved like wax. Shadows flowed over forms trying to hide under seats, absorbing them into cold nothingness, leaving only faint frost patterns behind. The monsters didn't stay confined. They surged out of the shattered Palace doors, flooding Main Street. The safe thrill was over. The horror was loose, hungry, and utterly real.

Chaos consumed the town. The stitch-faced man stalked alleyways near the diner, his laughter a wet gurgle. The insectoid thing scaled the bank building, shattering windows with its spiked legs, reaching in with dripping claws. Shadows pooled under streetlights, stretching into tendrils that snaked around ankles, pulling victims screaming into the deepening gloom. The hulking slasher methodically kicked in doors, his pipe finding hiding places behind sofas and inside closets. Alien shrieks, clicks, and tearing sounds echoed from rooftops and basements. People died on their porches, in their cars stalled in panic, hiding under beds that offered no sanctuary. The air filled with the coppery tang of blood, the sour stench of terror, and the unnatural chill radiating from the things that stalked the town.

A small group of survivors huddled in the looted hardware store. Jenna, her Palace uniform smeared with someone else's blood. Ben, the high school janitor, gripping a crowbar so tight his knuckles were white. Mrs. Pevensie, the librarian, face pale but eyes sharp. They saw Sheriff Dawes try to organize a futile defense near the town hall steps. He fired his pistol at the approaching slasher. The bullets sparked harmlessly off the metal mask. The pipe came down. They didn't watch the rest. "We can't stay," Ben said, peering through a crack in the boarded window. The street outside writhed with movement – shifting shadows, the glint of arthropods, the lumbering shape of the slasher moving towards the next house. "They're everywhere. They're hunting house to house."

"The police station," Jenna urged, voice trembling but determined. "It's brick. Reinforced doors. Maybe…maybe they have guns locked up. Real guns." It was a desperate gamble. They moved like ghosts themselves, through tangled backyards, over splintered fences, keeping to the deepest alleys filled with overflowing dumpsters. They avoided the lit streets where the shadows twisted with predatory life. They saw Mr. Evans, the Palace's ancient projectionist, stumble out of his vine-choked cottage, clutching a heavy, dented metal case close to his chest. He took two steps onto his weed-choked path. A shadow detached from his own, deepening, solidifying. It flowed over him like tar. He vanished without a sound, leaving only the case lying in the dirt. They ran faster, breath burning in their lungs. The sounds followed – skittering on rooftops, guttural breathing from unseen doorways, the distant, rhythmic *thud* of the slasher's pipe meeting resistance.

They reached the station. The heavy reinforced door was damaged but intact. Inside was chaos – desks overturned, papers strewn like confetti, dark stains on the linoleum floor. It was empty. The heavy steel armory door in the back stood slightly ajar. Rifles, shotguns, boxes of ammunition. A flicker of hope. "Barricade the front!" Ben yelled, grabbing a pump-action shotgun and shells. "Use everything! We hold them here!" For a frantic few minutes, they worked. They shoved metal desks against the door, piled heavy filing cabinets, wedged chairs and broken monitor stands into any gap. Sweat stung their eyes. Jenna found a heavy-duty backup generator humming in a cramped storage closet. It powered weak emergency lights and, crucially, the station's internal systems. Including a large monitor screen mounted on the wall in the briefing room, currently displaying static.

Suddenly, the main doors shook under a massive impact. Wood splintered near the deadbolt. The metal shrieked. "They're breaking in!" Mrs. Pevensie cried, fumbling with a heavy revolver. Ben racked the shotgun. "Get ready! Aim for center mass!" Another colossal crash. The barricade buckled inward. The doorframe cracked with a sound like breaking bone. Through the widening gap, Jenna saw the slasher's mask, blank and menacing, the insectoid thing's clicking mandibles dripping corrosive saliva, shifting shadows massing and pulsing behind them like a living wall. Mr. Evans' metal case lay near Jenna's feet, knocked over in their rush to barricade. It had sprung open. Inside wasn't a weapon. It was complex, unfamiliar equipment – strange lenses of smoked glass, copper coils, spools of film that seemed too dark, absorbing the light. Projectionist's gear. But not like any she'd seen at the Palace. It felt old, wrong, pulsing with a faint, icy vibration.

An idea, wild and desperate, struck her. The generator. The monitor screen. The Palace horrors came *from* the screen. Maybe...maybe this projector was different. Maybe it could send them back. "Ben!" she screamed, pointing at the equipment. Her voice cracked. "The projector! Hook it to the screen! Point it at them! Fast!" Ben stared, confusion mixing with terror on his face. The splintering door focused him. He grabbed the strange projector; it was unnaturally cold. Mrs. Pevensie helped him heave the surprisingly heavy device onto a cleared desk, aiming its lens directly at the large wall monitor. Jenna frantically connected thick cables from the humming generator to ports on the projector, then found matching ports on the monitor's side. The projector emitted a low, unnatural vibration that resonated in their teeth. Its lens glowed with a sickly, internal green light, but no image appeared on the screen yet. The air grew thick, cold, hard to breathe.

The main doors gave way with a final, rending crash. The barricade exploded inward in a shower of splinters and twisted metal. The slasher stepped through the wreckage, pipe raised, dripping red. The insectoid creature scuttled in behind him, clicking eagerly. Shadows flowed across the ceiling like spilled ink, dripping down the walls in viscous streams that pooled on the floor. Jenna fumbled with the projector's controls – dials marked with unreadable symbols, switches that hummed under her touch. "How does it work?!" Ben raised his shotgun, aiming at the slasher's chest. "Just turn it on! Point it at them!" Her fingers found a large, worn lever switch. She threw it.

The projector didn't cast light *onto* the monitor. The lens seemed to *pull*. The weak emergency lights dimmed further, their glow visibly sucked towards the machine. The air grew thick as syrup and bitingly cold. The projector's hum deepened to a bone-rattling drone that shook the floor. The advancing monsters paused. The slasher tilted his head, the mask turning towards the projector. The insectoid thing chittered, mandibles clicking rapidly, its multifaceted eyes fixed on the glowing lens. The pooling shadows on the floor stopped their flow, seeming to ripple towards the device. For a second, Jenna thought it was working. Repelling them. Ben lowered his shotgun a fraction, hope flaring in his eyes. Mrs. Pevensie gasped.

Then the slasher lowered his pipe. He took a step, not towards the survivors, but towards the projector. He reached out a gloved hand, not to smash it, but almost…reverently. The insectoid creature scuttled closer, a low, almost purring click coming from its thorax. The shadows on the ceiling condensed, forming a dark, elongated humanoid shape that drifted silently down towards the machine. They weren't afraid. They were *drawn*. Mesmerized. The projector's drone intensified, becoming a physical

4

pressure in their skulls. The large monitor screen flickered violently. Not with an image *from* the projector, but with a deep, swirling vortex of absolute darkness. Shapes moved within it – terrible, familiar shapes, writhing and pressing against the surface from the *other side*. More slashers. Swarms of insectoids. Legions of the stitched and the shadow-born. A disturbing mass of pure nightmare. The vortex pulsed, growing larger, deeper.

The slasher touched the projector's icy casing. The vortex on the screen bulged outward, distorting the monitor's frame. A new shape began to coalesce within the swirling dark – vast, indistinct, but radiating palpable, crushing dread. Larger, more grotesque, more fundamentally *wrong* than anything yet seen on Main Street. The drone became a shriek that vibrated their bones and threatened to burst their eardrums. Jenna understood. The projector wasn't a weapon. It wasn't a shield. It was a door. A beacon. A key turning in a cosmic lock. And they'd just turned it on *inside* their only refuge. They hadn't found salvation; they'd found the epicenter.

The slasher turned his blank mask towards the survivors. Behind him, the vortex on the screen bulged impossibly, the monitor's plastic casing cracking. The new horror within began to push through, a limb like petrified smoke testing the air of the station. Ben fired his shotgun. The blast was deafening in the confined space, but the sound was instantly swallowed, muted, by the projector's all-consuming scream. The pellets sparked harmlessly against the slasher's chest, leaving no mark. The station lights flickered wildly, then died completely, plunging the room into near-darkness. The only illumination came from the projector's hellish green lens and the monstrous, shifting shapes now fully emerging from the ruptured screen – entities of pure shadow and jagged bone, dripping void and whispering madness. Jenna's last thought wasn't of escape, but of the Palace's dark marquee, the eager crowds, the safe thrill. The horror wasn't contained. It never was. It just needed a door. The final frame closed not on darkness, but on the projector's relentless, hungry glow, pulsing in the silent, corpse-strewn ruin of the station, the vortex on the screen still churning, reaching out. The drone continued, a beacon now echoing across the empty town.

The Bottom of the Well

The rain hammered the kitchen window, just like that night. Martha flinched at a sudden crack of thunder. Across the table, Frank stared into his cold coffee, his knuckles white on the mug. Fifteen years. Fifteen years of silence, of pretending, of jumping at shadows. The phone rang.

A jolt went through them both. Landlines rarely rang anymore. Martha's hand trembled as she reached for the receiver. Frank's eyes locked onto hers, wide with a warning.

"Hello?" Martha's voice was thin.

Silence. Then, a woman's voice. Clear, calm, chillingly familiar despite the years. "Mom?"

Martha dropped the receiver. It clattered on the linoleum, the plastic casing cracking. The voice continued, tinny and distant from the floor. "Dad? Are you there?"

Frank surged up, kicking his chair back. He grabbed the receiver, pressing it hard to his ear. "Who is this?" His voice was a harsh rasp.

"It's me." The voice was older, steadier than the child's they remembered, but the cadence...it was *her* cadence. "Sarah. I'm...I'm okay. I think I'm coming home."

Frank's face drained of color. He looked at Martha, his eyes reflecting her own abject terror. They hadn't called her Sarah in fifteen years. They never spoke the name. Martha clamped a hand over her mouth, stifling a whimper. They *knew*. They knew with cold, sick certainty what they had done. The small body. The old well deep in the back woods. The shovel Frank had cleaned so meticulously.

"How?" Frank choked out. "Where are you?"

"It's hard to explain," the voice replied. There was no static, no distortion, just that calm, impossible clarity. "I remember...flashes. The rain. The dark. The smell of wet earth." Martha swayed, gripping the counter. She remembered the smell too, clinging to Frank's clothes when he came back inside alone. "I remember the well."

Frank slammed the receiver down. The silence crashed back, louder than the thunder. He braced himself against the wall, breathing hard. Martha slid down to the floor, hugging her knees, rocking.

"It can't be," Frank whispered, more to himself than her. "It *can't* be."

"It was her voice," Martha gasped. "Frank...she said the well."

"Some sick joke!" Frank snapped, turning on her. "Someone found something. Someone knows." Paranoia, thick and acrid, filled the small kitchen. Had they missed a button? A hair? Did someone see Frank walking back that night, covered in mud?

The phone rang again.

They froze. The shrill sound pierced the air like a knife. It rang once. Twice. Three times. Frank stared at it like a venomous snake. On the fourth ring, Martha crawled forward, her hand shaking violently. She picked it up.

"Don't hang up, Mom." The voice was still calm, but a new note entered—something cold beneath the surface.

"I'm close now," it said. "I've been climbing for a long time."

Frank backed away from the phone. Martha's breath came in short gasps.

"I see the kitchen window. I see you."

Martha turned. The rain-slick glass reflected only the dim room behind her. Then, a pale face slowly emerged on the other side of the window. Mud streaked its hollow eyes. Its mouth didn't move.

The phone fell from Martha's hand.

Outside, something started knocking on the glass.

The Hatchlings

The *thump...thump...thumping* under the floorboards started weeks ago. Tonight, it stopped. There was silence. For the first time in a while. Sarah froze, the pulse in her wrist *tap...tap...tapping* against her skin. A dry rustle slithered near the cracked wall. Not under. *Inside.* Her stomach cramped violently. She looked down. Movement rippled beneath her thin nightshirt. Not one bulge. Dozens. Small, hard lumps shifting, pressing outwards. The final *thump* echoed inside her own body. Tiny mouths bloomed through her skin. She finally screamed as the first hatchling tasted the air.

The Glass Trap

The old wooden house stood at the end of Hemlock Street, its peaked roofs cutting into the perpetually gray sky. Mara Sutton, horror writer, craved its isolation. It dripped with atmosphere. Boxes littered the echoing downstairs rooms. She explored, drawn upwards. The attic hatch resisted, then creaked open. A ladder unfolded with a puff of disturbed dust.

The air was thick and still, smelling of decayed wood and years forgotten long ago. Weak light filtered through a grimy circular window. Shapes loomed under dusty sheets: furniture, trunks, stacked paintings. Then she saw it, leaning against a far chimney, almost hidden. A tall, heavy mirror. Its ornate frame, tarnished silver or pewter, depicted twisting vines and strange, contorted faces. The glass itself was obscured by a thick gray shroud of dust and cobwebs.

Her writer's mind sparked. What stories did this glass hold? Who last looked into it? A thrill, the familiar itch of potential horror, pushed her forward. She reached out, ignoring the grime, and wiped the dust away with her sleeve. A wide swath cleared, revealing dark, surprisingly reflective glass beneath.

She saw herself. Her pale face framed by dark, messy hair pulled back. Wide, curious eyes. The reflection seemed...normal. Solid. Then it shifted. Not Mara moving, but the *image* behind her reflection. The dim attic wasn't empty anymore. Figures stood behind her spectral form in the glass. A woman in an old-fashioned maid's cap, eyes wide with terror. A young boy in shorts, mouth open in a silent scream. Others, indistinct but undeniably present, pressed close.

Mara gasped, stepping back. Her reflection didn't move. It remained in the center of the glass, but the background figures grew clearer, more desperate. The maid clawed at the air. The boy pounded tiny fists against nothing. Mara's reflection stared back at her, its expression shifting from curiosity to the beginning of abject horror.

Before Mara could turn, run, scream, the glass *lurched*. Not the mirror itself, but the surface. It became liquid, viscous, like dark mercury. It bulged outward towards her. A terrible suction pulled at her, not a physical wind, but an irresistible force emanating from the glass. It seized her breath, her muscles, her very will.

She stumbled forward, one hand raised instinctively. Her fingertips touched the cold, yielding surface. Instead of stopping, her hand sank *into* it. The cold shot up her arm, paralyzing. The suction intensified. Her reflection reached out too, its hand meeting hers *through* the glass. Their palms pressed together, separated only by the thin, impossible barrier. The reflection's mouth opened in a perfect mimicry of Mara's own silent scream.

The world tilted. The dusty attic, the weak light, the stacked belongings – they stretched, distorted, then snapped away like a rubber band. Mara felt a sickening lurch, a sensation of being pulled through a keyhole. Darkness swallowed her for a heartbeat. Then, light returned, but it was wrong. It was cold, flat, and emanating from everywhere and nowhere.

She stood in a gray, featureless space. Endless fog stretched in all directions. Silence pressed down, absolute and smothering. She whirled around. Behind her, a vast pane of glass showed the attic. Her attic. Exactly as she'd left it. The mirror frame surrounded the view like a window. She could see the dust particles in the weak light, the sheet-covered shapes, the chimney.

She was inside. Inside the mirror.

Panic detonated. She lunged at the glass, slamming her palms against its icy, unyielding surface. "NO!" The scream tore from her throat, raw and primal. It made no sound. The silence absorbed it completely. She pounded harder, fists beating against the barrier. She could see the attic floorboards inches away, the dust she'd disturbed. Freedom was *right there*, impossibly close, utterly unreachable.

Fingers touched her shoulder. Mara spun. The spectral maid stood beside her, tears streaking her translucent cheeks. She shook her head slowly, hopelessly. The little boy huddled nearby, knees drawn up, rocking silently. Other figures drifted in the gray fog behind them – a man in a suit, an old woman in a shawl, faces etched with the same eternal despair. Trapped souls. She was one of them now.

Mara turned back to the glass, pressing her face against it. She saw her own reflection now, but it wasn't *her*. It stood in the attic, exactly where she had stood moments before. It looked down at its hands, then touched its face – *her* face. It looked around the attic, a slow, curious smile spreading across its lips. A smile Mara never wore. It walked towards the ladder, movements confident, weary.

The reflection paused at the attic hatch. It looked back, not at the room, but directly *at* Mara trapped behind the glass. It met her frantic, terrified eyes. And it winked.

Then it descended the ladder, closing the hatch behind it. Mara slammed her fists against the silent glass until they bled, screaming soundlessly into the endless gray prison. Her reflection walked freely through her new house, wearing her skin. The mirror stood in the attic, its glass dark and waiting once more.

Last Call

The neon "Open" sign buzzed its final minutes. Rain streaked hard against the black windows. Ben wiped down the bar, the cloth scrubbing over polished oak. Empty stools, empty tables. It was almost closing time. Almost.

Except for the man in the corner booth.

He'd arrived near midnight. Sat alone. Drank steadily. Never spoke. Ben hadn't paid him much mind until the others left. Now, the silence pressed in, thick and uncomfortable. Only the rain and the low buzzing of the cooler broke it.

"Last call," Ben announced, his voice echoing slightly. He needed to clean the taps, lock up, get home.

The man in the booth didn't move. His suit, charcoal gray, looked expensive and perfectly dry despite the storm outside. He stared into his glass, half-full of an amber liquid Ben didn't remember pouring. The light above the booth seemed dimmer near him.

Ben walked over. "Sir? We're closing." He kept his tone polite, professional. Bar rules.

The man looked up.

Ben stopped. The eyes were dark. Too dark. Not brown. Black. Deep, endless black that swallowed the weak light. Ben felt a chill through his spine. Just tired, he told himself. Long shift.

"One more," the man said. His voice was smooth, low, like stones grinding underwater. It held no warmth.

"Kitchen's closed. Just drinks. And last call *was* last call." Ben gestured vaguely towards the door. "Time to settle up."

The black eyes fixed on Ben. A faint smile settled on the man's lips. "Settle up. Yes." He placed his glass down with deliberate care. "A final transaction."

He reached into his jacket pocket. Not for a wallet. He pulled out three coins. Ancient-looking. Heavy gold, maybe, but tarnished, scarred. They gleamed dully in the low light. He placed them one by one on the damp coaster beside his glass. *Clink. Clink. Clink.*

Ben stared at the coins. They felt...heavy. Heavier than they should have been. He cleared his throat. "Dollars are fine. Or card."

The man ignored him. He pushed the coins slowly towards Ben with a single, long finger. The nail was perfectly clean, sharp. "Payment rendered. For service." He paused. "And silence."

The chill intensified. The air grew colder. The buzz of the cooler seemed louder. Ben glanced at the door. Locked from the inside, but the deadbolt wasn't thrown yet. He could get there. "Look, pal, I don't know what game you're playing. Take your weird coins and go. Now."

The smile widened slightly. The black eyes held Ben's. "The game is concluded. Payment is made. The contract is sealed." He tapped the coins. "Pick them up."

Ben didn't want to touch them. They repelled him. But anger flared, hot and sudden, cutting through the fear. "Get out!" He slammed his hand down on the bar near the booth. "Or I call the cops!"

The man leaned back. He seemed amused. "Call them. See who arrives." He gestured again to the coins. "Pick. Them. Up."

Ben's hand moved. Almost against his will. His fingers brushed the top coin.

Fire. Ice. A jolt like electricity shot up his arm. He gasped, snatching his hand back. The coin clung to his fingertip for a split second before falling back onto the bar with a soft *thud*. Where it touched his skin, a tiny, perfect circle of flesh was gone. Vanished. Leaving only smooth, unbroken skin beneath, white and bloodless. No pain. Just absence.

Horror flooded Ben. He clutched his hand. "What are you?"

The man stood. He was taller than Ben realized. The shadows in the booth deepened, clinging to him like smoke. "The Settler of Debts. The

13

Keeper of Promises. The Last Patron." He took a step towards the bar. "You served. You were paid. Your silence is part of the fee."

Ben backed up, hitting the counter behind the bar. Bottles rattled. "I didn't agree to anything!"

"You took the coin." The man's voice was a whisper that filled the room. "You accepted payment. For service rendered. And for forgetting what walks the world when the lights go out."

He reached the bar. Placed his palms flat on the oak. Where his skin touched the wood, a faint, dark scorch mark appeared. Smoke curled, smelling of sulphur and old dust. "Your shift," the man said, those black eyes boring into Ben's soul, "is just beginning. A long one. Eternity, in fact. Serving drinks. Maintaining silence."

Ben saw it then. Not a man. Something else. Something vast and ancient and utterly cold wearing a human shape. The suit seemed less real, more like shadows stitched together. The rain outside sounded like distant screams.

"No!" Ben lunged for the baseball bat under the bar.

He was fast. The man was faster. A hand shot out, impossibly quick. Not a fist. An open palm pressed against Ben's chest, right over his heart.

No impact. No shove.

Just cold. Absolute, soul-freezing cold. It spread from the point of contact, icy tendrils snaking through muscle, bone, blood. Ben froze. Not paralyzed. Turned to ice from the inside. He couldn't move. Couldn't breathe. Couldn't scream. His vision blurred at the edges.

The man leaned close. Ben smelled death and decay. "Welcome," the low voice vibrated in Ben's frozen bones, "to the night shift. Forever."

The pressure vanished. The cold remained, locked deep within Ben's core. He collapsed against the back counter, gasping, shivering violently. He looked up.

The booth was empty. The coins were gone. Only the faint, fading scent of sulphur and the scorch marks on the bar remained.

The neon sign flickered and died. The bar plunged into near darkness, lit only by the emergency exit sign.

Ben pushed himself up. His limbs felt heavy, alien. The silence was absolute now. There was no rain, no buzz. Just the frantic pounding of his own heart, a sound too loud in the stillness.

He looked towards the door. He needed to lock it. Secure the bar. Start the closing routine.

His feet carried him behind the bar. His hands moved automatically. Polished the wood. Checked the taps. Wiped a glass. The motions were familiar, comforting. Routine.

He finished wiping the glass. Held it up to the dim green glow of the exit sign. It was clean. Perfect.

He placed it back on the shelf.

Then he turned. He faced the empty bar stools. The empty tables. The locked door. The silence pressed in, deeper than before. Eternal.

A customer would come. Eventually. When the world slept. When the real dark descended. He needed to be ready. To serve. To maintain the silence.

Ben straightened his apron. He waited. The cold inside of him was a permanent companion now. His first eternal shift had begun. The only sound was the slow, inevitable ticking of a clock counting down forever.

The Standing Man

Old Man Harris scanned the corn. Tall, green, rustling. His scarecrow stood as a sentinel in the center field. He called it the Standing Man. It had a rough wooden frame. A stuffed burlap sack head. Faded plaid shirt. It hadn't moved the crows lately. They perched on its arms, mocking.

Harris gripped his shotgun. He needed to check the far fence. The path led right past the Standing Man. He hesitated. Last week, his best dog vanished near that spot. Just...gone.

He pushed into the rows. The stalks closed around him, whispering. The air grew still, thick. He focused on the Standing Man's shape ahead. Its burlap face seemed darker. There was a rip where its mouth should be.

He reached the clearing around its post. The scarecrow stood as always. Yet...something felt off. The angle of the head? The drape of the shirt? Harris squinted. The burlap head seemed tilted. Watching him. He shook the feeling off. Just straw and rags. Nothing more.

He turned towards the fence line. A sound stopped him. A low, dry rustle. It wasn't corn. It was behind him.

He spun. The Standing Man faced him. Its head tilted the other way now. Impossible. The post was fixed. No wind stirred the heavy air.

Harris raised the shotgun. "Who's there?" His voice cracked. There was only silence. Then, a soft *thump*. A single crow fell from the sky, landing near his boots. Its neck broken.

Fear coiled in his gut. He backed away, keeping the gun trained on the scarecrow. It didn't move. Just stood, watching.

He reached the edge of the corn. Relief washed over him. He turned to run for the farmhouse.

A figure blocked the path. The Standing Man. Its burlap head was inches from his face. He hadn't heard it move. A smell hit him – dry rot, old earth, something metallic.

Harris jerked the shotgun up. Too late. Rough, straw-stuffed arms shot out. Hard as seasoned wood. They seized his shoulders. The grip crushed bone. He screamed. The sound died in the thick corn.

The scarecrow pulled him close. Up close, the burlap head wasn't smooth. Stitches formed crude features. Two dark button eyes stared, empty. Below them, a ragged slash opened in the sack. Not a mouth. A hole. A rip in the burlap. Dark and deep. It drew him in.

He fought, kicked. It was useless. The thing was immovable. The hole widened. He saw only darkness inside. A dry, rustling sound came from within, like countless insects stirring. It pulled his face towards the opening.

His scream was muffled by burlap. Then, silence. The corn rustled softly around him. The Standing Man released its grip. Old Man Harris slumped to the dirt, unmoving.

Later, his wife found the shotgun near the field. She called his name. There was no answer. She was filled with dread. She scanned the corn. Her eyes found the Standing Man. It stood tall in the center field. Its posture seemed...straighter, more defined. The faded plaid shirt looked different. It was bulkier, filled out. The burlap head seemed fuller, the crude features sharper. It faced the house. Watching.

She saw the boots. Thick work boots, caked in familiar mud, protruding from beneath the scarecrow's ragged pant legs. Boots her husband wore. She took one step forward, a hand flying to her mouth. The Standing Man's burlap head turned slowly, deliberately, fixing its dark button eyes directly on her. She froze. The field held its breath. The Standing Man watched. Waiting.

The Rescue

Part One

The forest swallowed the path behind Ben. His flashlight beam cut weak cones in the thick dark. Every rustle in the underbrush froze him. He shouldn't have taken the shortcut. Not tonight, not after the warnings. A low branch scraped his jacket like fingernails. He quickened his pace. His breath clouded the freezing air. Something heavy moved through the trees parallel to his path. It wasn't an animal, too deliberate, too quiet. He broke into a run. His boot caught a root. He fell hard, the flashlight spinning away, plunging him into absolute darkness. Silence. Then, slow, dragging footsteps approached from where he fell. Closer. Closer.

Part Two

Ben scrambled backwards on hands and knees, blind. The dragging sound stopped inches away. He felt hot, rancid breath on his face. He squeezed his eyes shut. A voice whispered, shockingly close to his ear. It sounded like his sister, Sarah. "Ben? Are you hurt? I found you." Relief flooded him. Sarah! He turned, reaching out. His hand touched rough, cold bark where her face should be. The voice chuckled, a dry, rattling sound utterly unlike Sarah. "Found you," it repeated. Strong, impossibly thin fingers clamped around his wrist like iron vines. The last thing Ben saw was the beam of his own flashlight, lying yards away, illuminating the empty forest floor as the creature pulled him into the suffocating dark.

The Passenger Seat

The headlights cut through rain. The road was empty. I drive fast, too fast.

Something thumps in the trunk. Not luggage.

My hands shake on the wheel. I shouldn't have looked in the farmhouse cellar. Shouldn't have taken the camera.

A shape flickers in the rearview. Closer than before. Ragged clothes. Skin like wet clay.

I floor the accelerator. The engine screams, trees blur.

Another thump. Louder. From the back seat this time. Cold breath hits my neck.

I spin the wheel. Tires screech. The car slides sideways, stops.

Silence. Rain hammers the roof.

I fumble for the camera. Maybe proof. I turn it on. Scroll to the last photo.

It shows me driving. Smiling. Something dark and long-fingered sits beside me in the passenger seat. Its hand rests on my shoulder.

The passenger door handle clicks open behind me.

The Heirloom

The ring felt unnaturally cold. Tarnished silver, it held a single, dark stone. Grandfather locked it away years ago. "Never touch it," he said before he died. Mother gave it to me yesterday. "Your burden now," she whispered, eyes hollow. She wouldn't meet my gaze.

I resisted. For hours. But the stone seemed to pulse in the dim light. A low humming sound that vibrated in my bones. My hand seemed to move without my permission. The ring slid onto my finger.

Ice shot up my arm. The humming sound became a voice, ancient and dry, inside my skull. *At last.* My body stiffened, not paralysis. Invasion. My legs stood. I moved. My feet walked me downstairs. My hand picked up the kitchen knife.

Mother sat in the parlor, staring at the empty chair where Grandfather used to sit. She didn't look up. My arm raised the knife. I fought. I strained every muscle. Sweat beaded on my forehead. The voice chuckled. I could hear it but I had no control.

Your blood weakens the seal. Your hand finishes the work. My fingers tightened on the knife handle. My body stepped closer. Mother finally looked at me. She saw the ring. Saw my eyes. Understanding, then terror, filled her face. She opened her mouth to scream.

My arm moved, swift, precise. The knife found its mark. Mother slumped. My hand released the blade. It clattered on the floor beside her. The voice inside me sighed, a sound unfamiliar. *Good. Now, find the next.*

I felt my lips curl into a smile. It was my own. The ring felt warm against my skin. My feet turned me towards the door. I walked out into the night. My hands opened the gate. My mind screamed inside a prison of flesh and bone.

The Face in the Glass

Martin ignored Mr. Hayes's warning. The caretaker's words about the attic device meant nothing now. The small, dark box on the workbench pulled at Martin. It felt cold, like polished stone. Specks of dust moved slowly through the weak light from the single dirty window.

Hayes had been clear: "Don't touch it. Don't look too long. Bad things happened here." He'd locked Martin in, a final precaution. "Safer that way," he'd muttered.

Martin switched on his penlight, not the regular beam but the one with the unsettling violet emitter. He aimed the purplish particles at the box's central disc. A low groan filled the air. The disc shimmered, then glowed a sickly pink. A shape began to coalesce within the glass – a blurred, pale oval. A face.

He wasn't alone. A man stood near the slanted wall, watching. Tall, gaunt, dressed in the blackest black he had ever seen. His skin looked unnaturally smooth, stretched tight. His eyes were dark pits. He didn't speak. He didn't move. He simply stared at Martin, then at the box. A terrible longing filled his expression.

The violet light intensified. The pink glow brightened. The face in the disc sharpened. Martin recognized the features forming. They were *his* features. Panic surged. He tried to pull the light away. It stuck fast. The hum became a shriek.

The gaunt man lunged, not at Martin, but toward the box. His thin hand plunged into the violet beam, into the glowing disc where Martin's face now shone clear. Agony tore through Martin's skull, a feeling of skin peeling, features dissolving. He screamed, but no sound came. The gaunt man's fingers closed within the light, pulling.

Martin watched, frozen, as his own face – his living, breathing likeness – detached from the disc like a mask made of light and shadow. The gaunt man held it. He raised it to his own blank, smooth head. It settled. It fused. It became his face.

The gaunt man blinked Martin's eyes. He smiled Martin's smile. He turned and walked silently down the attic stairs.

Martin stumbled to the small, tarnished mirror hanging near the window. He saw the smooth, blank oval where his face should be. Below it, the gaunt man's black suit now clothed Martin's own body. He touched the featureless skin. It felt cold. Final. Hayes's key turned in the lock downstairs. He was trapped. Faceless. The box sat dark and silent on the bench.

The Man at Dusk

He arrived with the fading light, a stranger stepping off the last bus. No one knew his name. He rented the old Miller place at the edge of town.

People noticed small things first. The stray cats vanished. Then Mrs. Hendrick's prize terrier didn't come home. A coldness seemed to follow the stranger. He smiled too wide, his eyes never quite matching the expression. He walked the empty streets after dark.

I saw him outside my window last night. He stood perfectly still under the old oak, staring up. Not at the house, at my window, my room. I froze. He tilted his head, a slow, unnatural movement. His shadow stretched long on the ground, sharp and blacker than the night around it. It didn't move like a shadow should.

Tonight, the power went out. Candles flickered in the wind. Silence pressed in, thick and heavy. A floorboard creaked downstairs. Not the usual house noise. This was deliberate, slow, heavy. It was approaching the stairs.

My door handle turned, slowly, without a sound. The hallway was pitch black. He filled the doorway, a darker shape against the gloom. His breathing was quiet, too quiet. I couldn't move. I couldn't scream.

He stepped inside. Moonlight sliced through the window. It fell across his face. His eyes reflected the light like an animal's. His smile widened. No teeth showed, just darkness.

"Found you," he whispered. His voice sounded rough and ancient.

He lunged. Not at me, at the corner, my shadow. His hand plunged into the dark shape I cast on the wall. Agony tore through me. I felt a horrible pulling, a separation. I watched my own shadow peel away from the wall, writhing silently in his grasp. He held it tight. My body crumpled, empty and cold. He folded the shadow like a dark cloth and slipped it into his coat pocket. Outside, no dogs barked. He walked back into the night.

The Whisper

The cold floor pressed against her cheek. She hid under the bed, her heart beating hard against her chest. Upstairs. Heavy footsteps. Slow. Searching, for something or someone.

She'd changed the locks yesterday. Felt safe. Until the back door splintered an hour ago.

A floorboard creaked directly overhead. Dust drifted down. She held her breath. Silence. Then, a low whisper, right beside the bed frame.

"Found you."

She froze. The whisper came from *under* the bed with her. Not upstairs.

The footsteps above stopped. The thing beside her shifted. She understood too late. There were two. The locks kept them all inside.

The Locked House

Arthur Benton secured the seventh deadbolt. He checked the boarded up windows for the hundredth time. The house seemed to hold its breath. Outside didn't exist. Not since the fire took Clara and the children. Only inside mattered. Only the thing inside mattered.

It lived inside the walls. He heard it scratching. He felt its gaze on his neck, cold and heavy. It wanted him dead. He knew this. Decades of vigilance proved it. Poison in his tea he smelled just in time. Floorboards deliberately weakened under his feet. A noose hanging from the attic beam one morning, made from his own rope.

Tonight, the scratching became frantic. A dry, insistent sound behind the plaster near his chair. Arthur gripped his fireplace poker. Sweat stuck his shirt to his back. He watched the wall. He watched a crack appear. Then, a fine dust sifted down.

He lunged, swinging the poker hard. Very hard. Plaster shattered. Only darkness stared back at him. Empty. Silence fell, thick and sudden.

Then, the front door creaked. Arthur froze. He *knew* he locked it. He always locked it. The deadbolts slid open, one after another. *Thunk. Thunk. Thunk.* The sound echoed like gunshots. The heavy oak door creaked inward.

Moonlight sliced across the dusty hallway floor. No one stood there. Arthur backed away slowly, poker raised. The familiar chill settled on his shoulders. The presence was here. It was stronger, closer.

He retreated into the parlor, his heart pounding in his chest. He saw the frayed rope still dangling from the attic hatch. He saw the worn armchair where he spent his days watching the boarded up window. He saw the dusty photograph of Clara and the children on the mantel.

He saw the empty chair where he sat. He slid the noose around his neck.

The rope above him tightened. The floorboard under his feet gave way. The world dropped away. He saw the photograph smile. Darkness swallowed him. The house sighed. The door clicked shut. Seven deadbolts slid home.

Silver Trap

The moon was full and bright. David felt the familiar ache deep in his bones. His skin tingled. He locked his cabin door. Too late. He was always too late.

He stumbled to the floor. His joints cracked and creaked. His muscles twisted and contorted. Fur ripped through his skin. His scream became a guttural snarl. Human thought drowned in primal hunger.

He smashed through the flimsy door. The cool breeze of the forest air hit him. Scents exploded. Deer. Rabbit. Man. Close. He followed the human trail, low and fast.

Light spilled from a cabin window. Old Man Henderson. David knew the scent. Easy prey. He circled the cabin, silent despite his size. The door was unlocked. Old Man Henderson should have known better.

He shoved it open. Henderson sat in his armchair, facing away. The smell of fear filled the room. It smelled sweet. David tensed to leap.

Henderson turned. Not with fear, with resignation. He held a worn, wooden box. "Knew it was you, David," he said. "Knew the moon."

David snarled, saliva dripping. He lunged. Henderson flung open the box. Not a weapon. Dust. Fine, gray dust. It filled the air between them.

David crashed into the cloud. Agony. Pure, searing agony. His fur smoked. Skin blistered. He howled, collapsing. Silver dust. Everywhere.

Henderson stood over him, holding the empty box. "My boy served with you," he whispered. "He knew what you became. He sent me this. For tonight." He looked at the squirming beast. "I've been waiting."

Last Meal

The hunger burned. Lena watched the man through his apartment window. He moved alone. Easy. She'd fed poorly last night; weakness threatened her edges.

She flowed through the unlocked door like smoke. He stood in the kitchen, back turned, humming. The scent of his blood filled her. It was potent, rich. Her fangs slid free.

He turned, holding a steaming mug. No shock. No scream. Just tired eyes meeting hers. "Lena," he said, voice flat. "Took you long enough."

Her predatory focus faltered. He knew her name. That was impossible. She lunged, a blur of speed. He didn't flinch. Her hand closed on his throat, cold against his warmth. She pulled him close, mouth opening.

He lifted the mug slightly. "Chamomile," he said. "With a twist. Wolfsbane. Very concentrated. Took weeks to source."

The words registered as her teeth pierced his neck. Hot blood flooded her mouth. Ecstasy. Then, a bitter tang beneath the copper. Sharp. Wrong. Wolfsbane.

She recoiled and dropped him. He slumped against the counter with a grim smile. Fire ignited in her gut, spreading, corroding her inside.

"Poison?" she hissed, clutching her stomach. Agony lanced through her veins.

"Slow," he gasped, blood staining his chin. "But thorough. You killed my sister last month. Took her blood. Now you have mine. Both of us...inside you," He coughed. "Enjoy your last meal."

The fire consumed her. Her vision blurred. She saw only his fading, satisfied eyes before the dark took her.

The Devil's Whisper

The first time it happened, Claire thought she was dreaming.

A small shadow stood beside her bed. The digital clock read 3:07 AM.

"Mommy?"

Claire blinked awake. Her son, Noah, stood motionless in the dark, his pajamas rumpled from sleep. His eyes were open, but his gaze was distant—fixed on something beyond her.

"Noah? What's wrong, baby?"

His lips parted. The words came out flat, toneless.

"I'm sorry. The Devil told me to."

Then he turned and walked out.

Claire sat up, her pulse was thumping. She followed him back to his room, where he climbed into bed and fell asleep instantly, as if nothing had happened.

She told her husband, David, in the morning.

"Kids say weird stuff when they're half-asleep," he said while flipping pancakes. "Remember when he swore he saw a clown in the closet?"

Claire watched Noah pushing syrup around his plate. He didn't seem to remember the night before.

But it happened again the next night.

Same time. Same hollow voice.

"I'm sorry. The Devil told me to."

This time, Claire grabbed his shoulders. "Told you to do *what*, Noah?"

His eyelids fluttered. His breath smelled faintly of something burnt.

28

"To open the door."

Then his body went limp. She barely caught him before he hit the floor.

David took it seriously after that.

They checked the carbon monoxide detectors. They interviewed Noah at his preschool. They even called a child psychologist, who suggested night terrors.

But Claire knew. Something was wrong.

She set up a baby monitor in Noah's room. The first two nights, nothing.

On the third night, the audio cut out at exactly 3:07 AM.

The screen showed Noah sitting up in bed. His mouth moved, but no sound came through. Then he stood and walked to the corner of the room.

He reached for something *just* outside the camera's view.

Claire ran upstairs.

Noah's door was locked—from the *inside*.

She pounded. "Noah! Open the door!"

Silence. Then a whisper, so low she almost missed it.

"It's too late."

David kicked the door open.

Noah stood facing the wall. His fingers traced symbols in the peeling paint—crude, jagged shapes that made Claire's stomach twist.

The air smelled like sulfur. Like something burning but there was no fire.

David grabbed Noah. The boy went rigid, then screamed—a sound too deep, too raw to come from a child's throat. It was him—but it wasn't.

The lights blew out.

In the dark, something moved.

Not Noah. Something *behind* him. A shape with too many joints, its breath rattling like dry leaves.

Noah's head tilted back. His voice wasn't his own.

"*You should have listened*."

David lunged. The thing caught him by the throat.

Claire heard bones snap.

Then the thing turned to her.

She ran. Made it to the car. Peeling out of the driveway, she glimpsed Noah in the rearview mirror—standing in the doorway, waving goodbye.

The police found David's body in the basement. His ribs had been cracked open. His heart was missing.

Noah was gone.

Claire moved across the country. Changed her name.

But every night at 3:07 AM, her phone rings.

The caller ID says **HOME**.

She never answers.

But sometimes, in the dead of night, she hears it—a whisper through the static.

"*Mommy? I'm sorry*."

Then the line goes dead.

Blackwater

The pond had always been there, dark and still, at the edge of Blackwater, Georgia. The townsfolk called it cursed, though none could say why. Children dared each other to touch the water, then ran home shivering. Old men spat into the dirt when they passed it.

Then the drought came.

For weeks, the sun baked the earth. The pond shrank, its black water receding like a slow, deliberate breath. The mud at its edges cracked open in jagged lines.

That's when they found the bones.

Jake Tully saw them first. He was twelve, skipping rocks where the water had pulled back. His stone hit something pale and smooth—not a rock. A skull.

The sheriff came. Then the coroner. They pulled seven skeletons from the mud, all small, all old. Too old for records.

That night, the first dog went missing.

Old Man Haggerty's hound didn't come home. They found its collar in the reeds, the metal buckle twisted apart.

Then the Thompson boy vanished.

His mother swore she saw him walk toward the pond at dusk. They searched the water, the woods. Nothing. They found nothing.

The town gathered at the church. Preacher Vaughn opened his Bible, but the words stuck in his throat before he could even speak. Outside, the winds picked up, carrying the smell of acrid pond water and something older.

Jake's father, Ray, took a shotgun to the pond that night. He stood at the water's edge, staring into the darkness.

The surface rippled. Not from the wind.

Something rose.

It wasn't a man. It wasn't an animal. It was tall, its limbs too long, its skin slick and black like the pond water. Its face had no features—just a hollow where a mouth should be.

Ray fired. The thing didn't flinch.

It moved toward him, fast.

The next morning, they found the gun and a boot, nothing else.

The town locked their doors. They nailed crosses to windows. It didn't help. Nothing helped.

One by one, they heard the knocking at night. A wet, heavy sound. Then the scratching. Then the screaming.

By the time the rains came, Blackwater was empty.

The pond filled again, smooth and still as glass.

Beneath the surface, something waited.

It was hungry.

And the next town wasn't far.

The Man in the Old Wooden House

The old wooden house stood beyond the town limits. The wind scraped bare branches against its warped siding. People avoided the overgrown path leading to its door. Stories spread through the town like a virus. Is it haunted? Maybe. The man inside killed his family? Could be. He's hundreds of years old? Who knew. The only known facts were, a man lived there, he stayed hidden and he only moved at night.

Tommy Benson dared himself. A full moon hung low and cold. He needed proof, not ghost stories. Proof about the man. He crept through the dead grass, heart pounding. The house loomed, there were no lights, no signs of life. A smell hung in the air—something pungent and sour, like old milk.

He found a loose board near the foundation, a crawlspace. It was darker than night inside. Tommy wiggled through. The dust was thick, it choked him. He landed on packed dirt. It was silent. He flicked his flashlight. The beam cut through the darkness. Spiderwebs draped like ragged curtains. Empty jars lined rough shelves. A workbench held rusted tools.

Then he saw the stairs. Rough planks leading up into the house. Each step creaked under his weight. The sound echoed too loud. He reached the top. A door stood ajar. He pushed it open.

Moonlight streamed through a grimy window, painting stripes on the floorboards. The room held little: a threadbare armchair, a cold stone fireplace, a heavy table. And in the corner, farthest from the window's light, stood a box. It was long, narrow and wooden, like a coffin.

Tommy caught his breath. The stories rushed back. *Only comes out at night. Hundreds of years old.* His hand trembled. He aimed the light at the box. It was simple wood, no carvings but the lid didn't fit flush. There was a gap.

He crept closer. The sour smell grew stronger here. His foot knocked a loose floorboard. The sound cracked the silence.

A rasp came from inside the box. A dry scrape, like bone on wood.

Tommy froze. His light beam shook on the coffin lid.

The rasp came again, louder. Followed by a low, guttural sigh. Not human, not animal. It was something else.

Panic seized Tommy. He stumbled back. His heel hit the loose board again. The noise was sharp, louder.

There was only silence. Then a slow, deliberate scraping *inside* the box. Like fingernails dragging along the underside of the lid.

He sleeps in a coffin. He sleeps in a coffin. The thought screamed in Tommy's head. He scrambled for the stairs, the light beam jerking wildly. He didn't look back. He plunged down the steps, through the crawlspace, out into the freezing moonlight. He ran until his lungs burned, until the town lights flickered ahead. He didn't stop until he slammed his own door shut, leaning against it, gasping.

He told his older brother, Mike. Wide-eyed, breathless. "He's in there! In a box! Like a…like a *vampire!*"

Mike scoffed. "Vampires? Grow up, Tommy." But Tommy saw the flicker of unease in his brother's eyes. The story spread. Whispers in the schoolyard. Nervous glances towards the old wooden house at dusk. *Tommy Benson saw the coffin. He heard it move.*

Three nights later, Tommy watched from his window. Torchlight flickered down the street. Not one or two, a dozen. Maybe more. Men gathered. Mike was among them, holding a heavy stick. Their voices were low, angry murmurs Tommy couldn't make out. Fear curdled in his stomach. He hadn't meant for this.

He slipped out the back door. He had to get there first. Warn the man? Stop Mike? He didn't know. He just ran, faster than before, cutting through backyards, the cold air tearing at his throat.

He reached the house as the mob turned onto the overgrown path. Their torches cast long, leaping shadows. Tommy ducked behind a thick oak, heart racing. He saw Mike's face in the torchlight, set and hard.

They surrounded the house. A rock smashed through a downstairs window, glass shattered. Another rock followed, then another. Thuds against the warped wooden door.

"Come out!" a man yelled. Others took up the chant. "Come out! Come out!"

Silence from the house.

"Burn it!" someone shouted. "Smoke the devil out!"

Tommy watched, frozen. Torches moved towards the dry, overgrown brush near the foundation. He saw the flicker catch, small at first, then hungry, licking up the brittle stalks towards the wooden siding. Smoke began to curl, thick and black.

The front door burst open.

The man stood framed in the doorway. He was tall, impossibly thin. He wore simple, dark clothes, worn and patched. His skin was pale as the moon above. He didn't hiss, he didn't bare fangs. He looked...old, terribly old and terrified. His eyes, wide and dark, scanned the ring of fire and angry faces. They held no malice, only a deep, ancient weariness, and now, raw panic.

The fire reached the house wall. Flames crackled, climbing the dry wood. Smoke billowed.

"He can't cross fire!" Mike yelled, brandishing his stick. "See! He's trapped!"

The man flinched back from the heat radiating from the burning siding. He looked at the flames creeping closer to the doorframe, then at the mob blocking his escape. His gaze swept past them, past Tommy hiding behind the tree, towards the dark woods beyond. A desperate longing filled his face.

"The upstairs!" Tommy whispered, remembering the coffin room window. It faced away from the mob.

The man seemed to think the same thing. He turned and vanished back into the smoke-filled doorway.

"He's running!" Mike roared. "Get him!"

The mob surged forward, ignoring the growing heat. They shoved through the front door, into the burning house. Tommy saw them vanish inside, heard their shouts echoing, mixed with the roar of the fire. Flames danced in the broken downstairs windows.

He ran around the side of the house. The fire hadn't reached there yet. He looked up. The grimy window of the coffin room was open. The pale man was halfway out, scrambling, coughing, his thin frame wracked with spasms. He dropped to the ground, landing awkwardly. He tried to stand, stumbled, fell against the house wall. He gasped for air, his eyes streaming from the smoke billowing out the window above him.

He saw Tommy. Not with hunger. With a desperate, silent plea. He tried to push himself up again, his limbs trembling violently.

Boots pounded around the corner of the house. Mike led the charge, his face smudged with soot, eyes wild. He saw the man on the ground.

"There! Get him!"

The man made a feeble attempt to crawl towards the dark tree line. Mike reached him first. He didn't use the stick. He kicked, hard. The toe of his boot connected with the man's ribs. A sickening crack echoed over the fire's roar. The man folded, a choked gasp escaping him.

Other men arrived. They didn't hesitate, sticks rose and fell. Boots thudded against flesh and bone. There were no roars, no curses now. Just the grim, efficient sounds of violence, punctuated by the man's short, wet gasps that grew weaker with each blow.

Tommy stood frozen. He watched the thin figure crumple. He saw the ancient terror in the man's eyes fade, replaced by a terrible emptiness as the blows rained down. The man didn't fight back. He couldn't. He just took it.

The fire reached the corner of the house. Flames licked at the dry grass near the man's outstretched hand. The mob stepped back, panting. Mike prodded the still form with his stick. It didn't move. Smoke thickened the air.

One of the men spat on the ground near the body. "Told you he was just a man. A sick one. Hiding out here."

Mike nodded, wiping soot from his face. He looked satisfied. "Got what he deserved. Living out here. Scaring folks." He turned, noticing Tommy for the first time. His expression hardened. "Get home, Tommy. Now. This ain't for kids."

Tommy didn't move. He stared at the broken shape on the ground. The firelight danced on the pale, still face. The wide, empty eyes stared past the flames, past the trees, towards nothing. No fangs, no monstrous strength. Just a dead man, killed by torches and boots and fear.

The sour smell of burning wood and something else filled Tommy's nose. Mike grabbed his arm, yanking him away from the heat and the sight. "I said *move!*"

Tommy stumbled. He looked back once. The mob was already dispersing, their torches bobbing away. The old wooden house burned bright now, a beacon in the night. The man lay small and broken at its edge, forgotten as the flames consumed his home. The only sound was the hungry crackle of fire and the frantic beating of Tommy's own heart. He didn't scream. He didn't cry. He just let Mike drag him away into the dark, leaving the fire and the silence behind.

The Last Broadcast

The radio crackled to life at 2:17 AM.

David jolted awake, his hand fumbling for the dial. Static hissed, then a voice cut through—low, strained.

"If anyone's listening...don't let it in. It mimics. It learns. It sounds like us."

The transmission cut out. Then Silence. Complete silence.

David rubbed his eyes. Some idiot's prank, probably. He switched off the radio and lay back down.

Five minutes later, a knock rattled his front door.

He froze. No one came out here. His cabin sat miles from town, buried in dense woods.

The knock came again—three sharp raps.

David crept to the door but didn't open it. "Who's there?"

A woman's voice answered. "Help me. Please. My car broke down."

Relief washed over him. Just a stranded traveler. He reached for the lock, then stopped.

The radio had turned itself back on.

The same voice from before whispered, *"It's outside."*

David's blood turned cold. The woman outside spoke again. "Hello? Are you there?"

The radio hissed. *"Don't answer."*

The doorknob twisted, slowly.

David stumbled back as the door creaked open. The woman stood there, her face pale, her smile too wide.

"You shouldn't keep people waiting," she said.

The radio screamed static. David lunged for it, desperate for another warning, but the woman moved faster.

Her fingers closed around his wrist. They felt cold—too cold, too smooth.

The last thing David heard was his own voice coming from the radio.

"Too late."

Then the transmission ended.

The cabin went silent.

The door swung shut.

No one heard from David again.

The Boy in the Walls

Oliver first met Billy in the dusty corner of his new bedroom. He was six, and the big, old house felt full of whispering shadows. Billy seemed nice. He had messy brown hair, wore striped pajamas, and liked the same dinosaur toys Oliver did. He was quiet, mostly. Oliver's parents, David and Sarah, smiled at his stories about his new friend. Typical childhood imagination, they thought, harmless.

But Billy was cold. Oliver noticed it when they sat together on the floor building block towers. A patch of air around Billy felt like opening the freezer. Oliver would shiver, pulling his sweater tighter. Billy never smiled.

The whispers started soon after. Not loud, just words breathed into Oliver's ear when he was alone. "*Your mommy loves you so much. Does she?*" or "*Daddy looks tired of you.*" Oliver would frown, confused, but Billy would just point at a toy, distracting him. Sarah noticed Oliver talking back to empty air more often, his voice sometimes sharp, defensive. "He's just playing," David reassured her, though his own smile faltered when he saw Oliver flinch at nothing.

Billy's games changed. He didn't want dinosaurs anymore. He wanted to play "*Hide and Seek Forever.*" He'd urge Oliver to squeeze into tiny, dark spaces: the cramped cupboard under the stairs, the narrow gap behind the heavy washing machine. "They'll never find you," Billy would whisper, his voice thin and eager. Once, Oliver got stuck behind the water heater, panicked tears streaking his face until David, alarmed by his muffled cries, pulled him free. Oliver blamed Billy. David blamed Oliver's imagination getting too vivid. Sarah felt a cold knot tighten in her stomach.

Then the drawings appeared. Oliver, who usually drew sunny skies and smiling stick figures, started filling pages with dark scribbled figures. One showed a small figure falling down a long, black well. Another depicted two stick boys: one smiling under a yellow sun, the other behind dark bars. Written in Oliver's clumsy writing beneath it: "*Billy sad. Billy wants out.*" Sarah found it crumpled under his bed. She showed David. "It's just a phase," he said, but his voice lacked conviction. He started researching "overactive imagination" online late at night.

Billy grew bolder. Oliver started sleepwalking. David found him standing silently at the top of the steep, uncarpeted stairs in the dead of night, staring blankly ahead. Another time, Sarah woke to find Oliver's bedroom window wide open, cold rain lashing in, Oliver standing on the ledge, his small body swaying. She screamed, yanking him back, sobbing. Oliver woke confused, mumbling, "Billy said the moon was close." David boarded the window shut the next day. They took Oliver to a doctor. The doctor suggested. "Stress from the move." Sarah didn't believe it.

The cold spot followed Oliver. It wasn't just in his room anymore. It lingered near him at the dinner table, making him shiver even with the heat on. David felt it once, a sudden, unnatural chill when he hugged his son. Oliver began speaking in a different voice sometimes – flat, older, resentful. "Why do *you* get warm milk?" the voice would ask Sarah, dripping with resentment. "Why does *he* get stories?" Oliver's own eyes would look distant, clouded.

Desperate, Sarah delved into the house's history. The previous owners were vague. The ones before that…records were sparse. Late one night, hunched over her laptop in the silent living room, she found it. A microfiche article from 1952: "*Local Boy, 7, Perishes in Tragic Neglect Case.*" William "Billy" Miller. Parents frequently absent, left him alone for days. Believed to have fallen down the old, boarded-up service shaft in the attic while searching for food. His emaciated body wasn't found for weeks. The address matched. Sarah's blood turned to ice. She showed David the article. The color drained from his face. This wasn't imagination. This was something festering in their walls, drawn to their son's warmth and life.

They decided to move. Immediately. Boxes appeared. Oliver seemed listless, anxious. Billy was furious. Objects started moving. Oliver's favorite mug shattered on the kitchen floor. Doors slammed shut by themselves. The cold became pervasive, a physical weight. Oliver's whispers to Billy became frantic arguments. "No, Billy! I won't!" he'd yell at the empty corner of his room, tears streaming. The attic hatch, long sealed shut, rattled violently one afternoon.

The night before the movers were due, Oliver seemed calmer. Too calm. He ate his dinner quietly. He hugged his parents tightly before bed. "Love you," he whispered, his voice small. Sarah tucked him in, her heart pounding with dread. She checked the locks on his window, the door. She and David sat awake downstairs, listening to every creak, every sigh of the old house.

Around midnight, a sound woke them. Not a crash, not a scream. It was a *song*. A thin, reedy, off-key rendition of "Twinkle, Twinkle, Little Star," drifting down from upstairs. It was Oliver's voice, but somehow different, lifeless, cold.

They ran, taking the stairs two at a time, David's flashlight beam jerking wildly. Oliver's bedroom door stood open. The room was empty. The freezing air bit their skin. The singing came from above. The attic hatch was open. The folding ladder was down. David's flashlight aimed upwards into utter blackness.

"OLIVER!" Sarah screamed, her voice raw with terror.

The singing stopped. Silence, thick and heavy as a shroud. Then, a small voice, Oliver's voice, but flat and chillingly devoid of fear, floated down: "Mommy? Daddy? Billy says it's my turn to hide forever now. He says it's dark and cold up here. Just like his turn was."

David scrambled up the ladder, Sarah right behind him, choking on dust and panic. The attic was a cavern of shadows, piled with decades of junk. The flashlight beam swept erratically. It landed on the far wall. The old service shaft. The rotted wooden planks covering it were splintered, pushed outward from the inside. A jagged, black hole opened wide.

Oliver stood near the edge of the dark opening. He was facing them, but his eyes were wide, blank, reflecting the flashlight beam like an animal's. He held his stuffed dinosaur loosely in one hand. Behind him, the blackness of the shaft seemed to pulsate. The air was so cold it burned their lungs.

"Oliver, step back!" David pleaded, his voice cracking. "Come to Daddy!"

Oliver tilted his head. A small, terrible smile formed on his lips. It wasn't his smile. It was a cruel, joyless twist. "Billy wants to play," Oliver said, but the voice was layered, another voice beneath it – older, harsher, filled with decades of bitter loneliness. "He wants *my* room. He wants *my* mommy. He wants *my* life."

He took a small step backwards. His heel scraped the crumbling edge of the shaft.

"NO!" Sarah lunged forward.

42

Oliver's smile widened, grotesque on his small face. "He says it doesn't hurt for long," the layered voices whispered. Then, with shocking speed, he spun around.

He didn't stumble. He didn't cry out. He simply stepped backwards into the absolute blackness of the open shaft.

David's scream mingled with Sarah's as they reached the edge, the flashlight beam stabbing uselessly down into the impenetrable dark. They heard only one sound rising from the depths: not a child's cry, but a dry, rasping chuckle that echoed in the cold, still air. It hung there for a moment, a sound of pure, jealous triumph, before fading into silence.

The beam of the flashlight trembled in David's hand, illuminating only the swirling dust and the jagged edges of the broken boards. Below, the darkness remained absolute and silent. On the dusty attic floor, just by the splintered edge, lay Oliver's stuffed dinosaur. Next to it, a single sheet of paper. A child's drawing. Two stick figures holding hands. One was colored bright yellow, labeled "Oliver." The other was scribbled over entirely in thick, furious black crayon, almost tearing the paper. Underneath, in Oliver's handwriting, but jagged and deep: *__MY ROOM NOW__*."

The Man Across the Way

James first noticed the old man in the apartment opposite his own. The building was old, the air thick with dust. Their windows faced each other across a narrow, grimy alley. The old man was always there. Sitting in a worn armchair by his window, silhouetted against the dim yellow light of a single lamp. He never seemed to read, never watched television. He just sat and stared.

Not out the window. Not at anything James could see. He just stared straight ahead, into the gloom of his own room. His eyes, when the light caught them just right, shimmered a red orb. Otherwise, they were still, dark pits. A stillness too deep. A darkness that didn't belong in a human face. James felt it first as a tingle on his neck, a coldness in his gut. He looked away, shaken. When he looked back, the old man hadn't moved.

He started watching. It began casually. Glancing across the alley while washing dishes. Noticing the old man was always there, day or night. The armchair never seemed to be empty. James timed him. Three hours one afternoon. The old man didn't shift, didn't blink, didn't sip from the glass of water beside him. Just that unnerving stillness. That stare.

Then the things started happening. Small things, unexplainable things. The light in James' bathroom flickered violently one night, plunging him into darkness just as he saw the old man turn his head towards his window for the first time. The power came back seconds later. The old man was staring straight ahead again. James' cat, a normally placid creature, hissed and arched its back, fur standing on end, whenever James carried it near the window facing the alley. It refused to look outside.

James woke one morning to find dead flies arranged in a perfect circle on his kitchen counter. Another time, the smell of sulfur, sharp and rotten, filled his hallway for hours, vanishing as suddenly as it came. He told himself it was old pipes, coincidence. But the feeling grew. The old man wasn't just odd. He was *off*. Deeply, fundamentally off, evil.

The thought solidified like ice: *The Devil*. Not a metaphor, not madness. The actual *Prince of Darkness*, sitting in a threadbare armchair across a dirty alley, watching the world decay. Who else could stare like that? Who else could make light fail and animals recoil? Who else would arrange dead flies? James felt a terrible certainty settle over him. He saw what no one else saw because he was *meant* to see. It was his responsibility.

No one else would believe him. The landlord, Mrs. Haversham, just shrugged when James mentioned the quiet old man in 4B. "Keeps to himself, pays on time. Harmless." Harmless? James knew better. The Devil was patient. The Devil was waiting. But for what?

James stopped sleeping. He watched the old man constantly. He sketched the window, the armchair, the shadowy figure. He researched. Ancient texts online, blurry photocopies from obscure books in the library basement. How do you kill the Devil? Silver? Holy water? A specific prayer? The answers were contradictory and vague. Fire seemed a constant. Fire purified. He read about ancient rites, binding rituals, the power of true names. He found nothing definitive, only fear.

The obsession consumed him. His work suffered. His friends stopped calling. He ate little. His reflection in the mirror grew gaunt, eyes burning with a feverish light. He saw the old man everywhere – a shadow darting down a street, a figure standing too still in a crowd. The city itself felt tainted.

He needed a weapon, something beyond steel. He aquired a silver candlestick from a thrift store, heavy and cold. He filled a glass vial with water from the font of a locked church, scooped hastily one midnight. He sharpened a kitchen knife until it gleamed, whispering verses he found online. He practiced entering the old man's apartment in his mind – picking the cheap lock, crossing the small living room, driving the blade home before those dark eyes could focus. He saw the old man smile in these fantasies. It was a dry, knowing smile.

The night arrived. James felt it in his bones. The air in his apartment crackled. The streetlights outside flickered erratically. The old man sat in his usual place, but tonight…tonight his posture seemed different, expectant. James clutched the silver candlestick. The vial of holy water burned a hole in his pocket. The knife felt heavy, cold against his wrist where he'd strapped it.

He moved like a ghost through his own building. The alley was deserted, filled with shifting shadows cast by the faulty lights. The back door to the old man's building yielded easily to his practiced fingers. The stairwell smelled of damp and decay. Fourth floor, apartment 4B. His heart beating hard in his chest. The beating, almost a distraction. He pressed his ear to the door. There was only silence, utter, profound silence.

He picked the lock. It clicked open with shocking ease. He pushed the door inward.

The room was exactly as he'd seen it from his window. Sparse, dusty. The worn armchair sat facing the window, away from the door. The single lamp cast its weak yellow pool. The old man was there, seated, still.

James stepped inside, closing the door softly behind him. The air was thick and cold. It smelled faintly of sulfur and something James couldn't identify, like dry earth in a deep cave. He raised the silver candlestick, gripping it like a club. He pulled the vial from his pocket.

"Turn around," James commanded, his voice tight with fear and fury.

Slowly, with an unnatural fluidity, the figure in the armchair turned.

It was the old man's face. Wrinkled with thin white hair. But the eyes…they were voids. Not dark, but *absences*. An absence of light, an absence of color, an absence of life. Places where light went to die and they held amusement, a deep, ancient amusement.

James froze. The certainty that had driven him here curdled into pure, icy terror. The silver felt suddenly inert, useless. The vial of holy water seemed laughable.

"James," the old man said. His voice was like dry parchment, rustling. It wasn't loud, but it filled the room, vibrated in James' teeth. "You took your time."

James tried to speak, to utter a prayer, a curse, anything. His throat locked. He took a step back. His heel hit the closed door.

The old man stood. He didn't rise like a man. He unfolded, impossibly tall, his shadow stretching across the ceiling, warping the walls. The weak lamplight seemed to dim further, retreating from his form. The air grew colder still.

"You saw," the thing that looked like an old man said. Its mouth didn't move quite right with the words. "A flicker. A glimpse behind the curtain. Few do. They see only the tired shell. You saw the tenant." It took a step forward. No floorboard creaked. "You thought…what? That I was some wandering fiend? A tempter in a cheap suit?" The amusement deepened, becoming cruel. "I am not *in* this place, James. I *am* this place. This building. This street. The rot in the walls. The despair in the hearts of those who dwell here. I am the slow decay you breathe every day."

James whimpered. The knife trembled in his hand. The silver candlestick felt like lead. The holy water might as well have been tap water. How do you kill the essence of decay? How do you stab the dark?

"I am not the Devil you read about," the thing continued, its voice weaving through the cold air. "I am older. Hungrier. I am the inevitable end that waits in the cracks, in the forgotten corners, in the weary sigh of existence. I am what happens when hope crumbles." It gestured with a hand that seemed too long, fingers like dry twigs. "And you…you brought yourself to me. You focused your fear, your rage, your fragile little light…right here." It smiled a smile that looked like a crack in old leather. "You made it so very easy to step out of the walls and *take*."

James lunged. Not with the knife. Not with the silver. He threw the vial of holy water. It shattered against the thing's chest. He drew the knife.

Nothing happened. The liquid darkened the worn fabric of the cardigan, nothing more. The thing looked down, then back at James. The amusement vanished, replaced by infinite cold. The void eyes fixed on him.

"Fool."

James screamed and stabbed forward with the knife. The blade sank into the cardigan, met resistance…then passed through as if the figure was made of smoke and dust. James stumbled forward, off-balance, crashing into the armchair. It was empty, utterly, completely empty. Cold dust puffed up from the fabric.

The lamp went out.

Darkness swallowed the room. Not the dark of night, but an absolute, suffocating blackness. James couldn't see his hand in front of his face. He couldn't breathe. The cold intensified, biting deep into his bones, stealing the air from his lungs.

A dry chuckle echoed around him, coming from everywhere and nowhere. From the walls. From the floor. From inside his own head. *"Thank you, James. Your fear is…exquisite. Your despair will sustain me. Your light is mine now."*

Panic exploded in James' chest. He scrambled blindly, hands flailing, searching for the door. His fingers touched wood, slick with something cold and damp. He clawed at it, searching for the knob. It wasn't there. Where the door should be, there was only smooth, unbroken wall, chillingly cold to the touch.

The chuckle came again, closer this time. A presence filled the darkness, vast, ancient and endlessly hungry. It pressed in on him from all sides. James opened his mouth to scream, but the cold rushed in, filling his throat, his lungs, turning his blood to ice. The last thing he felt was not pain, but a profound, absolute emptiness, a crushing weight of despair settling into the space where he used to be. The darkness claimed him completely. It had always been waiting. It had simply needed a key. James had delivered himself. The apartment across the alley remained dark. The armchair sat empty. In James' own apartment, the window facing the alley shattered silently inward, scattering glass like frozen tears across the dusty floor. The building sighed, a sound like settling bones. It had fed well.

The First Hunger

*...(for he that is hanged is accursed of God;)...(**Deuteronomy 21:23**)*

*And, behold, the veil of the temple was rent in twain from the top to the bottom; and the earth did quake, and the rocks rent; And the graves were opened; and many bodies of the saints which slept arose, And came out of the graves after his resurrection, and went into the holy city, and appeared unto many. (**Matthew 25:51-53**)*

I

The ground didn't just shake, it ripped itself apart. The sky went black at noon, not like dusk, but like ink poured over the world. Inside the temple, the thick curtain separating the Holy of Holies tore down the middle with a sound like a giant's final gasp. Outside, the earth convulsed, rocks split open with sharp cracks. Tombs, ancient and new, opened wide.

Silence followed. It was an unnatural, suffocating quiet. Then, movement. From the broken tombs, figures stirred. Not living men rising refreshed, but bodies pulling themselves from the cold earth. Dirt clung to burial shrouds. Skin, where visible, was gray, slack. Eyes, when they opened, held no life, only a terrible, vacant hunger. These were the saints who had fallen asleep, raised. But not to glory, to something else.

They shuffled from the graves. Their movements were stiff, jerky. They moved not towards light, but drawn by a scent on the wind, a pulsing warmth emanating from the walled city – Jerusalem. They moved as one, a ragged, silent procession of the dead. More joined them from other broken tombs along the way, pulled by the same instinct.

Three days later, the borrowed tomb near Golgotha yielded its occupant. The massive stone rolled aside, not by angels, but by a force from within. He emerged. The wounds were still there – the cruel punctures in hands and feet, the gash in his side. But the eyes...the eyes were wrong. Gone was the profound depth, the compassion. In its place, a flat, dull emptiness, reflecting the pre-dawn gloom like stagnant water. His movements, once purposeful, were now the same stiff, unnatural lurch as the others. He sniffed the air. He turned towards Jerusalem, the city that had condemned him. A low, guttural moan escaped his lips, echoing the sound now constantly rising from the horde converging on the city. He joined the shuffling mass. He led it.

II

Panic gripped Jerusalem like a fever. The stories were wild at first –
madmen escaped tombs, a plague of walking sickness. Then the screams
started. From the outer districts, then closer. People saw neighbors, relatives,
even revered figures known to be buried, shambling through the streets.
They moved slowly, relentlessly. They didn't speak, they moaned, they
grabbed and they bit.

And they ate. Not flesh. Brains. They sought the head, cracking
skulls with surprising strength, fingers digging into the soft matter beneath.
The streets ran slick with blood and gray matter.

Miriam huddled with her brother, Caleb, and a dozen others in the
back room of Ezra the potter's shop. The heavy wooden shutters were
bolted, shelves braced against the door. Outside, the moaning was a
constant, dreadful chorus. Thuds sounded against the walls as bodies
pressed mindlessly forward.

"They are *everywhere*," a woman whimpered, clutching a child.
"The market...they just...fell on people."

"It's *him*," said Josiah, a temple guard who'd fled his post. His face
was pale with terror and rage. "The Nazarene. He claimed to be the Son of
God, but God cursed him! Hung on a tree! Deuteronomy says it! Cursed is
everyone who hangs on a tree! Look what his curse has brought! He leads
them! I saw him! Empty eyes, shuffling like the rest, but *leading*!"

"Blasphemy!" cried old Rebekah, rocking back and forth. "He was
the Messiah!"

"Messiah?" Josiah laughed, a harsh, broken sound. "Does that look
like salvation? That's a walking curse! He brought the dead back, but not to
life! To *this*! God has abandoned us because we followed a false prophet!"

A heavy thump shook the door. Dust sifted from the ceiling.
Everyone froze. The moaning outside intensified, focused now on their
hiding place.

"They know we're here," Caleb whispered, gripping a heavy clay urn.

"Quiet!" Ezra hissed. "Bar the back door too! Move those sacks!"

They worked frantically, piling everything heavy against the doors and the shuttered windows. The potter's shop became a fortress of desperation. Outside, the thudding grew more insistent. Fingernails, or perhaps bone, scraped against the wood.

Days bled into a nightmare. The moaning never ceased. The pounding came in waves. They had little water, less food. Sleep was impossible. Every scrape, every thud, sent jolts of terror through them. They took turns watching the barricades, weapons in hand – Ezra's kiln poker, broken pottery shards, a stolen Roman short sword Josiah clutched like a talisman.

Miriam watched Josiah, his anger festered. He muttered about the curse, about the false messiah leading the dead. He sharpened the sword obsessively. "If I see him," he whispered once, catching Miriam's eye, "I'll put him back in the ground. Properly."

They heard screams from nearby buildings, abruptly cut off. The moans would grow louder in those places for a time, then return to their constant vigil outside the shop. The stench of decay and death seeped through the cracks in the shutters.

One afternoon, a section of the roof, weakened by the earthquake or the constant pressure below, groaned ominously. They all looked up, hearts pounding.

"They can't get up there, can they?" Rebekah asked, her voice thin with dread.

"They shouldn't be able to climb," Caleb said, trying to sound certain. "They just…shuffle."

But the groaning timbers argued otherwise. The relentless pressure was taking its toll, not just on their nerves, but on the very structure sheltering them.

III

The end came not with a roar, but with a splintering crack. It was deep in the night, during Miriam's watch. She was staring, hollow-eyed, at the main door, lit only by a single flickering oil lamp. The barricade shuddered. A central plank, stressed beyond endurance, snapped in two with a sound like a breaking bone.

A gray hand, fingers caked with dried blood and dirt, wiggled through the gap. Then another. They clawed blindly, tearing at the broken wood, widening the hole. A low moan, louder now, filled the shop.

"They're in!" Miriam screamed, scrambling back.

Chaos erupted. Sleepers jolted awake. Caleb grabbed Miriam, pulling her towards the back room. Ezra lunged forward with his kiln poker, jabbing at the grasping hands. Josiah screamed a wordless battle cry and thrust his sword through the gap. It struck something solid. A wet, crunching sound followed. The hands didn't withdraw.

More planks gave way. A head forced itself through the gap – a woman Miriam vaguely recognized from the fish market. Half her cheek was missing, revealing stained teeth. Her milky eyes fixed on Ezra. She moaned, a sound of pure, mindless hunger.

Ezra stumbled back, dropping the poker. Josiah slashed wildly with his sword, severing fingers that fell twitching to the floor. But more hands replaced them, pulling at the splintered wood. The gap widened.

A section of the barricade collapsed inward. Bodies tumbled through, landing in a heap of tangled limbs and ragged burial cloths. They didn't pause. They scrambled to their feet, their movements jerky but horrifyingly fast once the obstacle was gone. The stench of the grave flooded the room.

The survivors fought. It was brutal, messy, and utterly hopeless. Caleb swung his heavy urn, crushing the skull of a shambling man in priestly robes. Gray matter splattered the wall. The body collapsed, but two more lurched over it. Rebekah screamed as bony fingers closed on her arm. Josiah hacked at limbs, his sword biting deep, but the creatures didn't flinch, didn't bleed much, didn't stop. They only fell when the brain was destroyed.

Miriam saw Ezra go down, buried under three figures. His screams were muffled, then silenced. A child cried out, the sound cut short by a wet tearing noise. The oil lamp was knocked over, plunging the front room into near darkness, lit only by the moonlight streaming through the broken door. Silhouettes moved in the gloom, grappling, falling.

Caleb pulled Miriam into the back room, slamming the flimsy door and bracing it with his body. They could hear the feast beginning in the front room – the wet, crunching sounds, the low moans of satisfaction.

"The roof," Caleb gasped, eyes wide with terror. "The kiln chimney…maybe…"

They clambered onto the sturdy worktable. Caleb pushed open the small clay-encrusted hatch leading to the roof. The cool night air washed in. He boosted Miriam up. She scrambled onto the flat, tarred roof. Caleb started to follow.

The door behind him splintered. A figure stood there, silhouetted against the moonlight from the front room. It was taller than the others. Ragged strips of cloth hung from its body. Dark, matted hair framed a face shadowed by the moon behind it. But Miriam saw the wounds on the outstretched hands as it reached for Caleb. She saw the emptiness in the eyes that seemed to fix on her brother.

Caleb turned, bringing up a shard of pottery. The figure moved with sudden, terrible speed. It wasn't a lunge; it was a blur. One hand closed on Caleb's shoulder, the other shot towards his head. Caleb screamed, a sound of pure, primal terror.

Miriam acted without thought. She grabbed a loose roof tile, heavy and sharp. She screamed, a wordless challenge, and threw it with all her strength at the figure holding her brother.

It struck the figure squarely in the forehead. A dull, wet *thunk* echoed in the small space. The figure staggered back a single step, releasing Caleb. It turned its head slowly towards Miriam on the roof. The tile had embedded itself in its brow, just above those empty eyes. Dark, viscous fluid, not quite blood, oozed slowly around the clay edges. It didn't fall. It didn't even seem injured. It just stared at her with that profound, chilling void.

Caleb scrambled onto the roof, pulling the hatch shut behind him. He collapsed, gasping, clutching his shoulder where the thing's fingers had dug deep. Below, the moaning intensified. Thuds sounded against the hatch.

Miriam helped Caleb to the edge of the roof. The narrow street below was choked with figures. Hundreds...thousands...all facing the potter's shop, all moaning that single, awful note. They shuffled in place, packed tight, a sea of the dead waiting. Escape was impossible.

The hatch cover rattled violently. Then, with a splintering crash, it exploded upwards. The figure emerged first, the tile still lodged in its skull. It stepped onto the roof, moving with that unnatural, fluid speed. Behind it, others began to climb out, hands grasping the roof edge, hauling their dead weight up.

Caleb pushed Miriam behind him, raising his shard of pottery. It was pathetic, hopeless.

The figure with the tile in its head stopped a few feet away. It tilted its head, a grotesque parody of curiosity. The moonlight glinted on the ooze around the wound. It didn't attack. It just stared at Miriam, past Caleb. The empty eyes held no malice, no rage. Only that infinite, terrible hunger.

Miriam understood then. This wasn't a battle. It wasn't a curse from God or a punishment for following a false prophet. It was simply...feeding. The risen dead, led by the one they thought was their savior, were nothing more than an endless, ravenous hunger. The Messiah hadn't brought life, he had become the engine of an eternal, mindless consumption.

The figure took another step forward. Caleb lunged, screaming. His pottery shard scraped harmlessly against the thing's ragged tunic.

The hand shot out again, fast, brutal. Caleb's scream cut off abruptly, replaced by a wet, crunching sound.

Miriam didn't scream. She looked past the figure feasting on her brother, past the others now crowding the roof, towards the moonlit city. The moaning filled the world. There was no escape. No salvation. Only the First Hunger, and the endless night it brought. The figure finished with Caleb and turned its empty eyes, and the oozing wound in its brow, towards her. It took a shuffling step. The moan that escaped its lips was her name, spoken in a voice like grinding stones. She closed her eyes as the cold fingers brushed her hair. The hunger had found her.

The Night Wants Me Dead

Rain hit the city like nails on tin. The neon lights smeared across the soaked windows of my office. It was 2 a.m. when she walked in. Pale skin, dark coat, eyes like a knife wound. She didn't knock.

"I need your help," she said.

I looked at her hands. No ring. No shake. She was calm. Too calm.

"My sister's missing," she said. "Her name's Clara."

I lit a cigarette and waited. She watched me like a cat watches a dying bird.

"Clara vanished two weeks ago. Last I heard, she was staying in a motel on 8th. I think someone's after her."

"Cops?"

"They wouldn't listen."

"Why me?"

"You find people."

She slid a photo across my desk. Two women. Same high cheekbones. Same jet-black hair. One looked like trouble. The other looked scared.

"Why'd she run?" I asked.

"She saw something. She started talking nonsense. Said I wasn't who I said I was. Said I wasn't real."

She smiled, but her eyes didn't show it.

"I want her found," she said. "Before someone else does."

I took the job. I always take the job.

The motel on 8th was a hole in the wall. The desk clerk remembered her. Said she left in a rush, middle of the night. Left the room trashed. Said she screamed something about shadows crawling under the door.

I found a torn piece of notebook under the bed. It said, "She isn't my sister. She wears her face, but it's not her. It's wearing her skin."

I didn't sleep that night.

Next morning I checked hospitals, shelters, bars, anywhere a scared girl might run. Nothing. I called the client. She picked up on the first ring.

"She's running from you," I said.

"She's confused," she said. "She gets like that. Just keep looking. Don't go alone."

I followed leads into alleys that stank of rot and lies. Found a junkie who said he saw Clara a week ago, hiding in the tunnels under the train yard.

"She had a knife," he said. "Kept whispering she had to stay hidden. Said something was hunting her."

I went down into the tunnels. It was cold and wet and dead silent. I found a blanket, a cracked mirror, and a crude drawing scratched into the wall. It showed a woman with hollow eyes, sharp teeth, and long arms. Under it was one word: Sister.

When I climbed out, she was waiting. My client. Standing under the streetlight.

"I told you not to go alone," she said.

"You followed me."

"You're getting close. She'll run again."

"I think I believe her," I said.

"You don't even know what she is," she said.

Her face flickered. Just for a second. Her smile slowly faded, then returned slightly tilted. Her eyes glowed too bright. Then it was gone.

"You saw it," she whispered.

I didn't say a word.

She leaned in close.

"She lied to you. I am her sister. I'm the one who kept her safe all her life. And now she wants to burn it all down."

She walked away and vanished into the night.

I went back to my office and poured a drink. My hand shook. I looked in the mirror. My eyes were bloodshot. My face pale. I didn't recognize myself. I had to find Clara.

I followed rumors to a woman living in the ruins of a burned-out church on the edge of town. She was thin, wild-eyed. Knife on her belt. She stepped out of the shadows before I knocked.

"She sent you," she said.

"She hired me," I said.

"She wants me dead."

I believed her.

"She's not human," Clara said. "She was born in the dark. Wears faces. Becomes what you want her to be. That's how she feeds."

"Feeds?"

"On you. Your fear. Your need. Your love. She fed on me for years. I saw her true face once when I was a kid. Thought it was a nightmare."

"Why now?"

"She's growing. Wants more. You're next."

"I can help you. Protect you."

"No. You can't. You're already hers. She's marked you."

I felt it then. In my chest. In my bones. Like something watching from inside my skin.

"You're lying," I said.

"You think you're helping the good sister escape the crazy one. That's how she gets you. She makes you want to protect her."

She stepped back into the shadows.

"She'll come for me. You'll lead her here. You already have. So I'm leaving."

She vanished through a crack in the floorboards. I ran after her but the church creaked, and the stairs collapsed behind her. She was gone.

I stumbled back to my office. She was there, sitting in my chair, legs crossed, hands folded.

"You found her," she said.

"She ran," I said.

"Of course she did. She's sick."

"Maybe she's telling the truth."

Her smile faded.

"Then why are you still here?"

I didn't have an answer.

She stood and walked to me. I couldn't move. My muscles locked. My breath froze.

"You brought her scent back with you," she whispered. "That's enough."

She kissed me. My mind burned. I saw cities falling, skies bleeding, shadows crawling over everything. I saw my own face tear away like paper. I screamed but no sound came out.

Then she was gone.

I woke up two days later in a hospital. No wounds. No records. No explanation. Just a note: *She knows where I am. Don't come looking.* — *Clara*

I did anyway.

I chased her through basements, bus stations, rooftops, graves. Every time I got close, she disappeared. Every time, the thing pretending to be her sister got closer too.

I started seeing her in crowds. On street corners. Reflected in puddles. She whispered to me in dreams. Promised love. Promised truth.

One night I woke up in a motel, room spinning, blood on the mirror. I don't remember how I got there. She was lying next to me, watching me breathe.

"You belong to me now," she said.

I ran.

I found Clara again, living in the woods, inside an old hunting cabin. She looked older. Tired.

"She has your scent now," Clara said. "You led her straight to me."

"I want to stop her."

"You can't. But I can."

She opened a drawer. Inside was a small black box.

"This binds her. Seals her in the face she wears. I used it once before. I can do it again."

"Then do it."

"She'll kill you first."

"I'm already dead."

Night came fast. The cabin creaked. The air turned cold. Then the door opened.

She stood there. Her eyes were bottomless. Her mouth was wrong.

"Clara," she said. "You've always been jealous."

Clara didn't flinch.

"You're not my sister," she said.

She opened the box.

The thing screamed. Wind howled. Lights shattered. The walls cracked. I was thrown back. I saw her skin peel. Saw the thing inside. A mass of teeth, limbs, fire. Then silence.

Clara was gone.

The cabin was empty. The box lay closed.

I carried it with me for weeks. Slept in train stations. Couldn't trust anyone. Every face looked like hers. Every voice sounded like her whisper.

One night I opened the box.

She was inside, smiling.

"You never wanted her," she said. "You wanted me."

And I believed her.

Now I sit in my office. She's here again. In my head. In my blood. In my dreams.

I don't know if I ever found Clara. I don't know if I ever lost her.

All I know is the night wants me dead.

And she is the night.

Behind the Door

"Did you hear that?"

"No. What?"

"Scratching. From the closet."

"Don't start again."

"I'm not joking this time. Listen."

"Do you have a cat."

"No."

"Then it's the pipes."

"It's not the pipes. Go check."

"Why me?"

"Because I'm not opening that door."

"Fine. Nothing. Just coats."

"Wait…what's that smell?"

"I don't smell anything."

"Like wet dirt. And something else."

"Forget it. Let's go back to bed."

"You didn't close the door."

"I didn't open it."

"It's moving."

"I see it."

"Close it. Now."

"It won't shut. It's stuck."

"Something's holding it."

"Grab my arm. Pull me—"

"What is that? Oh God—what is that?"

"Don't look at it. Just run."

"I can't move."

"Don't look—don't—"

"It's in my head. It's talking."

"Pull away. Pull—"

"I can't. It wants me to stay."

"I'm calling someone."

"The phone's dead."

"Use your cell."

"No signal."

"Is this a dream?"

"No."

"Then wake me up. Please wake me up."

"Stay with me. Look at me. Don't turn around."

"I think it's closer."

"Don't look."

"Where's your hand? Where are you?"

"Still here."

"Whose hand is that on my shoulder?"

"Not mine."

"Tell me it's not—"

"Don't scream. Don't give it what it wants."

"It's whispering."

"What's it saying?"

"My name."

"How does it know your name?"

"I think…I think I've seen it before."

"When?"

"When I was a kid. In the basement."

"You never told me that."

"I never remembered. Until now."

"It's in the room."

"I know."

"Don't move."

"It's behind me."

"Don't look at it."

"I already did."

"Oh no."

"I think it followed me. All these years."

"Why would it wait?"

"It was waiting for you."

"For me?"

"It doesn't want me anymore."

"What does it want?"

"You."

"Why?"

"You saw it too."

"No I didn't."

"You did. Just now. That's all it needs."

"I don't understand."

"Neither did I. Not then."

"What happens now?"

"You go with it."

"I won't."

"You already are."

"I feel cold."

"It's inside now."

"Help me."

"I can't."

"Please."

"It's done."

"What?"

"You're not you anymore."

"Then what am I?"

"It,"

"No—"

"Yes."

"You lied."

"I had to bring someone."

"You used me."

"I'm sorry."

"Let me out."

"You can't come back."

"I don't want to be here."

"It's too late."

"I see the others."

"I know."

"They're screaming."

"Don't listen."

"You knew this would happen."

"I was alone. I couldn't take it anymore."

"So you gave me to it."

"Forgive me."

"I can't."

"I understand."

"I hope it takes you next."

"It won't."

"Why not?"

"I'm already part of it."

The closet door creaked shut.

The Dust Never Settles at Midnight

The sign creaked on rusted chains: *Midnight*. Cyrus Kane reined in his dusty mare at the edge of town. Night had fallen hard, but Midnight pulsed with an unnatural energy. Light spilled from saloon windows, piano music echoed thinly, and shadowed figures moved along the boardwalk. It looked alive. Too alive for this stretch of barren territory.

Kane dismounted, the worn leather of his holster creaking. His eyes scanned the street – the saloon, the general store, the livery, the hotel. All open, all lit. People talked, laughed, called out. Yet, a tingle touched his spine with the breeze. The air felt still, thick. No crickets sang, no night birds called. Only the sounds of the town, sharp and contained.

He stabled his horse at the livery. The old man there moved slowly, deliberately, his eyes avoiding Kane's, fixed on the task. "Quiet night," Kane offered.

The man just grunted, handing Kane a ticket. His skin looked papery in the lantern light.

The hotel desk clerk was equally taciturn. He was pale, they were all pale. Kane signed the register – the only fresh ink on a page filled with faded, identical names. "Room at the end. Quiet side," the clerk murmured, sliding a key across the worn wood. His fingers were cold when they briefly touched Kane's.

The saloon was the heart of the noise. Smoke hung thick in the stale air. Men played cards with intense focus. Women in faded finery served drinks, their smiles not showig in their eyes. Kane ordered a whiskey. It tasted flat, lifeless. He found a spot at the bar, observing. The conversations were loud, but disjointed. People spoke of cattle prices and dry weather, but their gazes flickered towards the windows, towards the deep dark beyond the town's lights. No one mentioned the day, no one spoke of sunlight.

He joined a poker game. The players were skilled, their movements economical. They barely spoke, their faces impassive masks under the low-hanging lamps. Kane won a few hands, lost a few. The coins felt strangely cold. He caught one player, a man with sharp features and eyes like chips of black marble, staring not at his cards, but at the pulse point in Kane's neck. Kane met his gaze. The man looked away, a muscle twitching in his jaw.

The night wore on. The piano player never faltered. The drinks kept coming. The crowd thinned only slightly. Kane felt a profound weariness seep into his bones, deeper than trail fatigue. It was a seductive pull towards sleep. He excused himself, leaving his winnings on the table. No one seemed to care.

Back in his hotel room, the silence of the hallway pressed in. He locked the door, checked the window – it overlooked a dark alley. The bed looked inviting. He lay down, expecting the usual restlessness, the hyper-vigilance of a man with a price on his head or a past that haunted him. Instead, a deep, dreamless sleep claimed him instantly. The best sleep he'd had in years.

Sunlight stabbed through the thin curtains, waking him. He stretched, feeling oddly refreshed. It was too quiet, the constant murmur from the saloon was gone. The clatter of wagons, the shouts of children – absent. It was utter silence.

He dressed quickly, holstered his Colt, and stepped into the hallway. It was empty, the lobby was deserted, the desk clerk gone. He pushed open the hotel doors.

Midnight was a ghost town.

Dust devils swirled lazily down the main street. Doors hung open, swinging slightly in the hot breeze. Windows gaped dark and empty. The saloon doors creaked forlornly. Not a soul stirred, not a dog barked. The vibrant town of the night had vanished. Only dust and silence remained.

Kane walked the length of the street. The general store: empty shelves, a layer of undisturbed dust. The livery: his horse stood alone, nickering softly. The blacksmith's forge: cold. The church: doors barred. He called out. His voice echoed, swallowed by the vast emptiness. Where had they gone? How could hundreds vanish without a trace before dawn?

He searched houses. Neatly made beds, cold fireplaces, tables set for meals never eaten. No signs of struggle, no signs of flight, just…emptiness. As if everyone had simply stopped existing at sunrise.

The heat of the day pressed down, oppressive. Kane felt watched, though he saw nothing. He retreated to the hotel, barricaded his door, and waited.

As the last sliver of sun vanished below the horizon, the sounds began. A door creaked open nearby. Footsteps on the boardwalk, a low murmur of voices. Then, the piano started up in the saloon.

Midnight was alive again.

Kane watched from his window. The same figures emerged from shadows, from buildings. The sharp-faced gambler. The pale barmaid. The slow-moving liveryman. They moved with purpose now, gathering, talking, their eyes glittering in the lamplight. Normalcy resumed, but the illusion was shattered. This wasn't a town. It was a performance.

The next day repeated the eerie emptiness. Kane stopped searching houses. He started searching for *where* they went. Cellars yielded nothing but cobwebs and stored goods. The church basement held only dusty hymnals. He checked the undertaker's – empty coffins on display, nothing hidden.

Desperation gnawed at him. He waited until the town was fully active the following night, then slipped out the hotel's back door. He moved like a shadow, avoiding pools of light, sticking to alleys. He needed to see where they came *from*.

He watched the saloon. Men emerged, but none seemed to arrive from a specific hidden location. They just…appeared on the street. He circled the church. Nothing. Then, near the edge of town, he saw her – the barmaid from the saloon. She left the noisy light and walked purposefully towards the small, neglected cemetery on the hill overlooking Midnight.

Kane followed, keeping his distance. The cemetery was overgrown, markers leaning or broken. The barmaid didn't stop at any grave. She walked to the back, to a crumbling stone mausoleum, its iron door hanging slightly ajar. She glanced around, then slipped inside.

Kane waited. Minutes passed, she didn't come out. He approached cautiously. The mausoleum door creaked as he pushed it wider. Inside, it was pitch black and the air was stale and dry. He struck a match.

The flickering light revealed not a burial chamber, but a set of rough stone stairs leading down into the earth. Cold air flowed upwards. Kane drew his Colt. He descended.

The stairs opened into a vast, low-ceilinged cavern. The matchlight barely pierced the gloom, but it glinted off polished wood. Rows upon rows of simple, sturdy coffins filled the space, arranged neatly on the dirt floor. Hundreds of them. The air was thick with the scent of turned earth and that peculiar, heavy stillness he associated with deep caves and sealed tombs.

His match died. Darkness swallowed him. But in that brief illumination, he understood. Coffins, not graves. They slept below. The entire town slept below his feet by day. Vampires.

The revelation hit him like a physical blow. The unnatural night life. The daytime desertion, the pallor, the cold. The staring eyes fixed on his neck. The flat whiskey. The deep, unnatural sleep he'd experienced – perhaps their presence induced it, kept prey docile. Midnight wasn't a town. It was a nest.

He needed to get out. Now. Before sunrise trapped him above ground with them waking beneath him. He backed towards the stairs, fumbling for another match. His boot scuffed a coffin lid.

A dry, rustling sound came from his left. Then another, right in front of him. Like stiff cloth shifting. A lid creaked. Slowly, agonizingly.

He struck the match. The flame flared, illuminating a coffin lid sliding open. A pale hand gripped the edge. Then a face emerged – the sharp-featured gambler from the poker game. His black marble eyes fixed on Kane, reflecting the tiny flame. A slow, predatory smile stretched his lips, revealing sharp, white points where his canine teeth should have been.

"Visitor," the gambler rasped, his voice like dry leaves.

Other lids began to creak open. Pale faces turned towards the light. Low hisses filled the cavern. Kane didn't hesitate, he fired.

The Colt roared, the sound deafening in the confined space. The bullet slammed into the gambler's chest. The impact jerked him back into his coffin. Kane saw the hole, dark liquid welling. But the gambler didn't cry out. He didn't fall. He pushed himself back up, the smile wider, crueler now. The wound smoked faintly but didn't bleed much. It didn't stop him.

"Lead won't kill us, gunslinger," the gambler hissed, climbing fully out. "Only slow us.

Kane fired again, twice. One shot took the gambler in the shoulder, the other grazed his temple. He staggered but kept coming. Others were emerging now – men, women, even children with dead eyes. They moved with that same deliberate slowness, but their numbers were overwhelming. They fanned out, blocking the stairs, surrounding him. Their eyes glinted with cold hunger.

Kane emptied his Colt. Bullets tore through cloth and pale flesh, knocking figures back, splintering coffin wood. But they rose again, or were replaced by others climbing from their boxes. The wounds closed slowly, smoking, but they didn't stop. The cavern filled with the stink of gunpowder and that ancient, earthy decay.

He was backing towards a wall, reloading with shaking hands. He was too slow. The gambler lunged, unnaturally fast. Kane dodged, but bony fingers raked his arm, tearing cloth and skin. Cold fire spread from the scratches. He kicked out, connecting solidly, sending the vampire crashing into a stack of coffins but more pressed in.

He got the cylinder loaded, snapped it shut. He fired point-blank into the face of a woman reaching for him. Her head snapped back, a ruin of bone and dark fluid. She collapsed, twitching. Finally down. Silver? Did it have to be silver? He didn't have silver bullets.

He fired again, taking down a man clawing at his leg. Another shot winged a child-vampire leaping from a coffin. They kept coming, relentless. Silent except for the hissing and the scrape of feet on dirt. He was running out of bullets, out of space.

He saw the barmaid near the stairs, her eyes fixed on him, a cruel smile on her lips. The exit. He had to reach the exit. He fired his last two rounds, clearing a momentary path towards the stairs, knocking two vampires aside. He bolted.

He scrambled up the stone steps, taking them two at a time. Cold hands grabbed at his ankles, his coat. He kicked wildly, feeling bone crunch under his boot heel. He burst out of the mausoleum into the cool night air of the cemetery. Freedom. He could run for his horse…

He skidded to a halt.

They filled the cemetery. Standing silently among the headstones, blocking the path down to the town. Dozens of them, hundreds, the entire population of Midnight. They stood perfectly still, watching him with those empty, hungry eyes. The gambler emerged from the mausoleum behind him, wiping dark fluid from his chin, his chest wounds still smoking. The barmaid stood at the front of the crowd, smiling.

Kane stood panting, his back to the mausoleum wall, his empty Colt heavy in his hand. The night was vast and silent, yet choked with their presence. There was no escape through that sea of pale faces and glittering eyes. No horse could outrun them all. He was cornered. The gunslinger, out of bullets, out of tricks, facing an enemy his weapon couldn't kill.

The gambler stepped forward. "Good run," he said, his voice a dry whisper. "Strong blood. It calls to us."

He gestured towards the crowd. "Join us. The hunt is eternal. The night is forever."

Kane's mind raced. Death was certain. A bullet to his own head? Quick. Clean. Or…become like them? A predator in the endless night? The scratches on his arm burned with unnatural cold. He looked at the sea of dead faces, no pity there, only hunger and a terrible, ancient patience.

He looked at his Colt. It was useless metal. He dropped it into the dust. The sound was final.

He looked back at the gambler. "How?" His voice was hoarse.

The smile widened, revealing the full length of those sharp, white fangs. "The Kiss," the gambler hissed. "It is a gift. And a curse."

The barmaid drifted forward, her movements liquid and predatory. Her eyes locked onto his. The crowd parted slightly, forming a path. Not towards the town, towards an open, empty coffin laid beside a fresh-dug mound of earth near the edge of the cemetery. His grave, already prepared.

"No running now," the gambler murmured. "Accept the night."

The barmaid reached him. Her hand, cold as marble, touched his cheek. Her eyes held no warmth, only that bottomless hunger and a strange,

73

terrifying invitation. She tilted her head, exposing the pale column of her own neck for a fleeting second, a mockery of vulnerability, then her gaze dropped to his throat. Her lips parted.

Kane closed his eyes as the cold descended, not just around him, but within him. The choice was made. The gunslinger was gone. Midnight had claimed its newest citizen. The dust would never settle for him again. The hunger began.

The Shaking Place

The snow fell not in flakes, but in thick, relentless sheets. It wasn't natural snow. It fell straight down, never drifting, piling in perfectly even layers that defied the howling wind only they seemed to feel. Frostbite crept under doorframes despite roaring fires. Food dwindled, hope dwindled faster.

Then the tremors started. Not deep, rumbling quakes, but sharp, violent jolts. Shelves emptied. Plates shattered. The ground beneath Frostwood heaved like a living thing, throwing people to their knees. Windows rattled in their frames, threatening to explode inward. Each tremor brought fresh terror and deeper snowdrifts, sealing doors, trapping people inside their homes.

"It feels like the world's breaking," Mary, the baker, whispered, clutching her daughter as another violent shudder rocked the small community hall. Dust rained from the rafters.

Worse than the tremors and snow was the *thing*. It came after the third big shake. No one saw it clearly at first. Just glimpses: a shadow too tall and thin, moving impossibly fast between the swirling white. Then the screams started. Old Man Hemlock found torn apart near the frozen creek, his cabin door ripped from its hinges. Two children vanished from a sled near the treeline, only bloody drag marks left behind. Fear became a living presence, colder than the storm.

"We have to leave," Kalvyn, the blacksmith, declared, his face grim in the lamplight. "This valley is cursed. The tremors, this snow...that *thing* hunting us. We head south, over the Whitecap Pass."

A desperate group formed: Kalvyn, Mary and her daughter Lara, the trapper Elvan, and a few others. They packed sleds with what little remained – furs, tools, precious tins of food. They left Frostwood under a sky filled with falling white, the tremors making the ground lurch beneath their snowshoes.

They walked for days, guided by Elvan's fading memory of the pass. The snow fell, harder. The tremors came, sharp and disorienting. The thing followed. They heard it sometimes – a skittering crunch on the snow behind them, a low, guttural clicking that froze their blood. One night, it took Jenna, the weaver. They found only her scarf, shredded and stained.

Finally, they reached where the pass should be. Instead, they found a wall, not rock, not ice. It was something smooth, cold, and utterly clear. It curved upwards, vanishing into the swirling white above. Kalvyn touched it. Glass. Perfectly transparent, impossibly hard glass. They followed it. It curved, always curving, enclosing them. Trapping them in a space far smaller than they ever imagined.

"No," Mary breathed, pressing her hands against the barrier. "This can't be. The world...the world is bigger than this."

A tremor hit, fiercer than any before. The ground bucked violently. The glass wall vibrated with a deep, resonant hum. Through the distortion, shapes moved on the other side. Vast, blurred shapes. Colored masses that shifted. A flash of movement that might have been a hand. A dark shape that could have been a face, peering in.

"People?" Lara whispered, pointing. "Are there people out there?"

But they were giants. Moving in a space filled with strange, enormous objects – towering green shapes like impossible trees, square mountains of color. The sight was incomprehensible, terrifying.

"Trapped," Elvan said, his voice hollow. "Like insects in a jar."

The realization crashed over them. Their entire world, Frostwood, the valley, the forests – all contained within this impossible glass sphere. The tremors weren't earthquakes. They were *shakes*. The unnatural snow? Debris stirred by the shaking. The monstrous thing hunting them? Another prisoner. And outside...a world they couldn't comprehend, populated by beings who might as well be gods.

The demon found them at the barrier. It flowed out of the blizzard, a nightmare of shifting shadow and bone-white fragments that seemed to ripple and distort with every vibration of the glass. It had too many limbs, or too few. Its mouth was a jagged tear filled with needle sharp teeth. It moved with the jittery speed of a spider, unaffected by the deep tremor currently rattling the snow globe.

Kalvyn roared, swinging his hammer. It passed through the thing like smoke, striking the glass with a dull *clang*. Elvan fired his rifle. The bullet sparked against the barrier, leaving no mark. The demon lunged. Its claw, cold and sharp as obsidian, ripped through Elvan's furs and chest. He fell without a sound, blood steaming on the snow.

Panic erupted. The survivors scattered. Mary grabbed Lara, running parallel to the glass wall, searching for a flaw, a crack, anything. The demon flowed after them, silent, relentless. Another tremor shook their world. The snow globe lurched violently. Mary and Lara were thrown against the glass. The impact knocked the breath from Mary. Lara screamed.

Through the vibrating glass, Mary saw it clearly this time. A child. A human child, impossibly large, its face pressed close to the curve. Curious eyes, magnified by the distortion, stared in. A small hand reached towards the snow globe, fingers splayed.

"No!" Mary screamed, pounding the glass with her fists. "Don't! Please, don't shake it!" But her voice was silent in that vast outside world.

The child's hand closed around the base of the snow globe.

The tremor that followed was catastrophic. The ground inside heaved like a stormy sea. Snow lifted in blinding clouds. The glass barrier screamed with strain. Mary saw a hairline crack appear, snaking upwards from the base near where they huddled.

The demon shrieked – a sound of pure, alien fury that cut through the shaking. It wasn't hurt, it was *excited*. It scuttled towards the crack, its form blurring, becoming less solid, more like concentrated smoke and darkness.

"It's going for the crack!" Kalvyn yelled, staggering towards it, hammer raised again, desperation in his eyes. "We have to stop it!"

He swung wildly as the demon reached the cracking glass. The hammer passed through its insubstantial form. The demon pressed itself against the crack, darkness oozing into the fine line. The glass groaned.

The child outside lifted the snow globe. It shook it. Gently at first, then harder, laughing at the swirling storm inside.

Inside, hell broke loose. The world became a violent, disorienting spin. The crack widened with a sharp *snap*. Ice-blue light, cold and sharp, pulsed from the widening crack. The demon shrieked again, a sound of triumph now, pouring its shadowy essence into the breach.

Kalvyn lunged, not at the demon, but at the crack itself, trying to block it with his body. The darkness touched him. He froze. His eyes widened in silent agony, then clouded over, turning flat and black. His skin grayed, withering in seconds. He crumpled, a dried husk, as the demon flowed over and through him, squeezing through the ruptured glass.

Mary clutched Lara, frozen in terror. The crack was big enough for a person now. Outside, the child stopped shaking. It held the snow globe up, peering in with wide, innocent eyes. It saw Mary and Lara pressed against the glass, faces etched with terror. It saw the gray, withered thing that was Kalvyn. It didn't see the shadow pooling on its own bedroom carpet, flowing from the base of the snow globe, darkening the fibers, beginning to rise.

Mary saw. She saw the darkness coalesce behind the child, taking shape in the shadows of the oversized furniture. The child, fascinated by the tiny people and the broken glass, remained oblivious.

The demon was out. It was free. In the child's world.

Mary pulled Lara away from the crack, away from the view of the oblivious giant child and the horror forming behind it. There was nowhere to run inside the shattered snow globe. The tremors had stopped. The snow settled into a grotesque parody of peace. The monster was gone but its freedom meant their doom was sealed. They were trapped in a broken ornament, waiting for the next shake, the next curious glance, or simply to freeze or starve. Outside, in a world of soft carpets and warm light, the shadow behind the child stretched taller, blocking the lamplight, and the child finally turned, its smile fading into a puzzled frown. The last thing Mary saw before the child moved away, taking the light with it, was the first glint of needle teeth forming in the rising dark. Escape wasn't freedom. It was just a different kind of feeding ground. And the shaking place was now utterly, silently, hopelessly still.

All Hallows' Feast

The air smelled of candy corn and woodsmoke. Orange pumpkin buckets swung from small hands. Liam, seven and dressed as a blur of red and blue (a "superhero," he insisted), bounced ahead. Chloe, four in a fuzzy unicorn onesie, clutched her mother's leg, wide eyes taking in the spectacle. Mark held Chloe's other hand, Sarah kept Liam in sight. Maple Street was alive. Jack-o-lanterns grinned from porches, fake cobwebs draped bushes and everywhere, monsters.

A hulking werewolf with disturbingly matted fur passed them, its low growl sounding suspiciously real. A trio of witches cackled over a cauldron filled with dry ice fog; one seemed to actually stir the air with her finger, the fog swirling unnaturally. A vampire in a pristine cape offered Liam candy; his smile revealed sharp, pointed teeth that looked less plastic, more bone. Liam hesitated, then grabbed a chocolate bar.

"Great costumes this year," Mark murmured, scanning the crowd. Sarah nodded, but a tingle touched her neck. The vampire's eyes had followed Liam a little too intently. Not hungry for candy, just hungry.

They turned onto Elm Street, more monsters. A ghost floated by, its sheet shimmering, feet not quite touching the pavement. A group of demons with latex horns and red body paint argued near a mailbox; the paint looked wet, glistening under the streetlight, and one demon flexed clawed fingers that dug grooves into the mailbox metal. Liam pointed. "Look, Mom! Scary!"

Chloe whimpered. "Too scary."

A clown with a cracked grin and disturbingly fluid movements approached Chloe. "Pretty unicorn," it rasped. It reached a white-gloved hand towards her horn. Chloe screamed, burying her face in Sarah's legs. The clown's hand stopped inches away. Its painted smile widened. Its eyes, behind the greasepaint, were utterly black.

"Hey!" Mark stepped forward, putting himself between the clown and his family. "Back off."

The clown tilted its head. It didn't move. Mark felt cold air radiating from it. Liam tugged at his sleeve. "Dad...its teeth..." Behind the painted red smile, the teeth were long, yellowed, and needle-sharp. Real teeth, not plastic.

A shriek tore through the night, close. Not a playful Halloween shriek, a sound of pure terror. Down the block, near a house decorated like a giant spider web, a werewolf wasn't play-growling anymore. It had pinned a teenager dressed as a zombie against a tree. Its massive jaws clamped down on the teen's shoulder. The sickening crunch of bone carried clearly. Blood sprayed the fake cobwebs, turning them crimson.

Silence fell for a heartbeat. Then chaos erupted.

The cackling witches stopped stirring fog. Their heads snapped towards the feeding werewolf, then towards the crowd. Their eyes glowed green. One pointed a gnarled finger, not at the werewolf, but at a family dressed as pirates trying to flee. "Fresh meat!" she screeched, her voice no longer human.

The vampire near Liam hissed, dropping its candy bowl. Its fangs extended fully. It lunged, not for candy, but for Liam's throat. Mark yanked Liam back, the vampire's claws ripping through the superhero cape instead. Sarah scooped up Chloe, screaming.

It wasn't costumes, none of it. The werewolves were tearing flesh. The witches were conjuring actual sparks of sickly green light. The ghosts drifted *through* solid objects. The demons' claws tore into screaming people. The monsters were real and they were hunting.

"Run!" Mark yelled, grabbing Sarah's arm. They bolted, dragging Liam. Behind them, Maple Street became a feeding ground. The air filled with screams, snarls, inhuman shrieks, and the sounds of tearing. The friendly Halloween decorations looked like grim premonitions.

They cut through backyards, stumbling over pumpkins and discarded decorations. Liam sobbed, struggling to keep up. Chloe wailed in Sarah's arms. Every shadow writhed. Every rustle promised teeth. They saw glimpses: a mummy unraveling its bandages to reveal dried out gray flesh beneath, wrapping around a fleeing woman; a group of goblins dragging a man into a sewer grate; a headless horseman, its pumpkin head burning with actual fire, riding down a screaming couple.

80

"Where are the people?" Sarah gasped, tears streaming down her face. "Our neighbors...the Andersons...?"

They rounded a corner onto a quieter street. A single house glowed with warm light. A man stood on the porch, waving frantically. He looked normal, human. "Here! Quickly! Inside!"

Hope surged. They sprinted for the porch. As they reached the steps, the porch light flickered. The man's friendly smile slowly changed to a frown. His eyes reflected the light like a cat's. He held the door open, but the inside wasn't a hallway. It was a yawning blackness that smelled of death.

Mark skidded to a halt, pulling Sarah and Liam back just as clawed hands reached from the darkness inside the doorway. The man on the porch laughed, a guttural, unnatural sound. His skin rippled, features melting into something scaled and reptilian.

"Keep moving!" Mark yelled, pushing them away from the trap. They ran blindly, direction lost. The entire neighborhood was a nightmare. Houses burned. Monsters feasted in the streets. No sirens sounded, no help came. Were they the only humans left?

They ducked into an alley behind the closed hardware store. Mark pressed them against the cold brick wall, listening. Snarls and screams echoed nearby, but the alley seemed empty, for now.

"What happened?" Sarah whispered, rocking Chloe. "Why is this happening?"

Liam sniffled. "The monsters are real, Dad. They're eating everyone."

A low growl rumbled from the far end of the alley. Eyes like hot coals gleamed in the darkness. A massive shape detached itself from the shadows – the werewolf from Elm Street. Blood matted its fur. Its muzzle was crimson. It sniffed the air, catching their scent. It lowered its head, muscles bunching.

"No," Mark breathed.

The werewolf charged. It covered the distance fast, too fast. Mark shoved Sarah and the kids behind him, raising his fists but it was futile. The beast leaped.

A blur slammed into the werewolf from the side. A vampire, the one who had lunged for Liam earlier. It crashed into the werewolf, snarling, fangs sinking into the thick fur. The werewolf roared, twisting, claws raking the vampire's back. They rolled, a whirlwind of fangs and claws, tearing at each other inches from the terrified family.

"Go!" Mark seized the chance. They scrambled out the other end of the alley, the sounds of the monstrous fight echoing behind them.

They found themselves near the edge of town, by the old, abandoned church. Its doors hung open. A faint light flickered inside. Candles? Desperation overrode caution. They ran up the steps and inside.

Dozens of faces turned towards them. Human faces. Pale, terrified, but human. People huddled among the pews. Relief washed over Sarah so powerfully she almost collapsed.

"Thank God," an older woman whispered. "More survivors."

A man with a bloodied bandage on his arm stood up. "Barricade the doors! Quickly!" Others moved, dragging heavy wooden pews towards the entrance.

Mark helped, his heart pounding with fragile hope. They blocked the main doors and the side entrance. The church felt safer, solid. Candles flickered on the altar, casting long, dancing shadows.

"We thought we were alone," Sarah said to the woman, holding Chloe close.

The woman shook her head, tears in her eyes. "They came when the sun went down. Just...changed. Or revealed themselves. We don't know. We hid. Some of us made it here." She gestured to a group near the altar, praying fervently. "Father O'Leary is trying to bless the grounds. Hold them back."

Mark joined the men reinforcing the barricades. Liam sat with other shell-shocked children. Chloe fell asleep in Sarah's arms, exhausted by terror. For a moment, the frantic pounding of their hearts eased. They had found sanctuary. They had found others.

A heavy thud hit the main doors. Then another. Wood splintered.

"They found us!" someone screamed.

The pounding intensified. Multiple impacts. The heavy pews shuddered. The barricade wouldn't hold.

Father O'Leary stood before the altar, holding a cross high. "By the power of the Lord, I command you unclean spirits—"

The stained-glass window above the altar exploded inward. Not from an impact outside. From *inside* the church.

A figure coalesced from the shattered glass fragments, hovering in the air. Tall, skeletally thin, draped in tattered robes the color of dried blood. Its face was hidden deep within a hood, only two points of cold, blue light visible. It held a twisted staff that pulsed with dark energy. A demon, not a costume, not a trick-or-treater. This was something older, hungrier.

The praying group near the altar screamed. The blue lights under the hood fixed on Father O'Leary. The demon raised its staff. The priest gasped, clutching his chest. His skin turned gray, withering before their eyes. He collapsed, a dried husk, the cross clattering to the stone floor.

Chaos erupted. The survivors scattered, screaming. The main doors burst open under the onslaught from outside. Werewolves, vampires, goblins, and twisted things with too many limbs poured in. The sanctuary became a slaughterhouse.

Mark grabbed Liam. Sarah clutched Chloe. They ran for the only exit left – a small door near a back room. A vampire lunged, Mark kicked it back, buying seconds. They burst through the door into a small, cluttered office.

There was no exit, only a high, narrow window.

The sounds of feeding and dying filled the church beyond the door. Snarls grew closer. Claws scraped wood.

"Up!" Mark lifted Liam towards the window. "Climb! Sarah, push Chloe!"

Sarah boosted Chloe up. Liam scrambled onto the narrow sill. Mark shoved Sarah up next. He turned as the office door splintered. The reptilian creature from the porch trap filled the doorway, its jaws open, dripping saliva. Behind it, the hooded demon drifted, its blue lights fixed on Mark.

Mark grabbed a heavy candlestick. He threw it with all his strength. It passed harmlessly through the floating demon. The reptilian monster hissed and surged forward.

"Go!" Mark roared at his family. "Don't look back! RUN!"

He turned to face the monsters, buying them seconds. Sarah pulled Chloe through the window, tumbling onto the damp grass outside. Liam followed. They ran into the dark field behind the church, towards the woods.

They didn't see Mark fall. They only heard the wet tearing sounds start before they were even halfway across the field. They didn't stop. They ran into the woods, branches whipping their faces, the sounds of the feast fading slightly behind them. They ran until their lungs burned and Liam stumbled, falling to his knees in a small clearing.

Sarah collapsed beside him, pulling Chloe close. They huddled together, listening. Only the wind in the trees. There were no screams, no snarls. There was just the wind and the distant, chilling toll of the church bell, ringing once, twice...marking the hour.

They were alone. Utterly alone. The woods pressed in. The wind sounded like whispers. Sarah looked down at Chloe, still in her unicorn onesie, her face streaked with dirt and tears. She smoothed her daughter's hair. Her hand brushed against the base of the cheap, glittery unicorn horn glued to the hood.

It felt warm. Solid. Not plastic. Almost...bony.

Sarah froze, she looked closer. The horn wasn't glued anymore. It seemed fused. Part of the fleece. Part of...Chloe?

Chloe looked up at her mother. Her eyes, usually bright blue, reflected the moonlight with a faint, unnatural silver sheen. A tiny, sharp point pressed against her lower lip. It wasn't a tooth, it was something new, something sharp.

Sarah's blood turned to ice. She looked at Liam, gasping for breath beside her. His ripped superhero cape clung to his shoulders. Was it clinging? Or...growing? His fingernails looked longer, darker, like claws in the dim light.

The wind sighed through the trees. It wasn't the wind. It was the voice of the hooded demon, whispering from the shadows just beyond the clearing. "The Feast...has only begun. The Change...welcomes all."

Sarah pulled her children closer, not knowing if she was protecting them, or protecting the world from what they were becoming. The moonlight filtered down, cold and unforgiving, illuminating the small clearing where the last humans huddled, waiting for the dawn that might never come, feeling the monstrous new life stirring within their own bones. The real horror wasn't just outside. It was taking root inside. All Hallows' Feast had claimed its newest offerings.

The Mud Beast

The mud sighed. Cold. Clinging. First his boots vanished.

Don't panic. He shifted. The sucking deepened. Thighs swallowed. *Wrong.*

He thrashed. A desperate heave. Mud surged to his chest. It pulsed. It pulled. Not earth. *Hunger.*

Gasping, he arched. Thick sludge filled his mouth. His nose. His eyes. The world narrowed to thick, cold pressure. The last bubbles burst silently on the surface. Smooth. Still. As if he'd never been. The mud sighed again. Waiting.

The Drowning Room

They told Maren not to swim out past the rocks. Everyone in town said the same thing. The signs on the pier didn't just warn about currents— they warned about vanishing.

Maren didn't believe the stories. She didn't believe in curses, or hauntings, or the quiet grief in her grandmother's eyes when she spoke of the bay. She just believed in water, and how good it felt to move through it. The ocean was the only place she didn't feel watched.

She walked down to the beach that evening alone. The sand was cold. The tide had pulled in deeper than usual. The surface of the water looked like dark glass, shimmering. She stepped in anyway.

No moon, no stars, just the wind and the slap of waves.

She waded out, careful, silent, focused. Her feet brushed across smooth rocks, then empty water beneath. She kicked forward, floated, let the salt sting her eyes. Ten feet. Twenty. Farther.

Then she saw them.

Figures in the water, five or six. No splashing, no sound, just rising. One stood fully, chest above the surface, arms limp. Another, closer, barely visible except for a head that leaned too far to the side.

Maren froze. She tread water, heart pounding. She whispered, "Hello?" The word barely made it out over the surface of the water.

They didn't move.

She blinked. The closest one began walking toward her.

Its legs didn't break the water. Its chest rose as if lifted. Its arms hung straight. Its head tilted toward her but no face showed. The skin was dark, shadowed, like it had soaked for years.

She turned and swam, hard, fast. Each stroke felt heavier than the last. Her limbs ached like something gripped them. She looked back. The figure was closer. Behind it, more were rising. They didn't swim, they floated, yet moved forward.

Her feet touched sand. She ran, she didn't stop until she reached the dunes.

When she looked back, the water was empty.

She told her mother. Her mother said nothing, just locked the door. Her grandmother prayed. Her father opened a bottle and didn't speak all night.

That night Maren heard the water in her room.

She lived on the second floor.

She sat up in bed, frozen. The floor glistened. Wet footprints trailed from the door to her bed. Then they vanished.

She didn't sleep.

The next day, she went to the library. The local history section was thin, dusty, mostly ignored. But she found what she needed.

There were drownings every few years. Always in the same area, past the rocks. Victims ranged from teens to adults. Some bodies were never recovered, some washed up days later, bloated and gray.

But once, in 1974, ten bodies surfaced at once. None were missing persons. No one recognized them. They looked almost identical—smooth faces, shallow sockets, no teeth. No autopsies, the coroner closed the report citing "decomposition and marine predation." The file didn't say who buried them.

Maren made copies. She kept them folded in her pocket.

At night, the water returned.

She woke to soaking sheets, her hair dripping. She hadn't moved. Her windows were locked.

She checked the floor. It was wet, then dry within minutes.

The dreams came next.

She walked down a hallway. Doors on each side. Water up to her knees. The light above flickered, humming.

She opened the first door. A child stood inside, back turned. It was motionless. The room was flooded to the ceiling.

The next door. A woman sat in a chair, submerged up to her shoulders, eyes open and empty.

Door after door. Room after room. People. Silent. Waiting.

She woke gagging, choking on water. Her sheets were soaked. Her skin pale.

The next morning, she went back to the beach. It was low tide and the rocks were slick with moss.

She waited.

Then she stepped in.

The cold bit deeper this time. Her legs numbed as she waded. She went farther, past where she saw them.

The water stilled. It was quiet.

She whispered, "I know you're here."

The surface broke behind her.

She turned. One figure rose, then another, then five, Ten, twenty. They were all watching.

They began walking toward her.

She didn't run.

She let the water rise over her mouth, her nose, her eyes.

Then she opened them underwater.

She saw them clearly now. Their faces weren't blank. They were hers.

Each one. Dozens of her. Different expressions. Some screamed, some smiled. Some stared, lifeless.

One reached for her ankle. Another touched her shoulder. The cold was gone.

Then she was standing.

But not on the beach.

A room stretched ahead of her. The walls rippled like water. She couldn't breathe, but she didn't need to. Everything was submerged.

She walked.

Door after door.

She opened one.

She stood inside it.

She looked at herself. The real her. Lying in her bed. Eyes shut. Breathing shallow.

She screamed, but the room didn't shake. Nothing changed.

She pounded on the glass. There was no sound.

Then she heard footsteps.

Behind her, the others stood. Silent. Waiting.

One pointed.

The water around her pulsed. The floor dropped. She fell.

She woke.

In her room.

Dry.

Sunlight poured in. Birds chirped. Her skin was warm.

She sat up.

Then she saw the photos. The ones she copied. Laid out on her desk. Every figure in the 1974 picture had her face.

Every one.

She blinked. Her reflection in the mirror shimmered.

Her mouth didn't move when she spoke.

She screamed but there was no sound.

She tried the door. It was locked.

She turned. The room stretched. Water pooled beneath the bed.

The walls breathed.

Outside, the town moved on.

People went missing, sometimes. The ocean took them.

But no one remembered Maren.

No one remembered any of them.

They stood in the water, waiting.

Still.

Quiet.

Watching.

The Monstrosity
Under the Stairs
Has Found a New Home

The house rules were simple. Unbreakable. No one goes near the room under the stairs after dark. Never open that door. Never shine a light inside. Leave a bowl of raw meat scraps just inside the kitchen door every Tuesday and Friday before sunset. Ignore the scratching. Ignore the low, growl sounds. Ignore the smell. Pretend it isn't there.

The Miller family followed the rules. They had for twelve years, since moving into the old house on Cedar Street. Sarah and David enforced them with quiet desperation. Their children, eight-year-old Lily and ten-year-old Ethan, learned fear before they learned multiplication. They knew the thing under the stairs was theirs. It was their burden, their mostly silent, hungry lodger.

Life rotated around that room. Furniture placement was set to minimize paths past it. Nightlights dotted the hallways, creating islands of safety away from its shadowed door. Conversations hushed near it. Laughter felt risky. They lived carefully, politely, like tiptoeing around a sleeping bear they knew wasn't really asleep.

The scratching started first. Not the usual scratching of claws against wood, but a slow, deliberate *dragging*. Like something heavy being moved inside the cramped space. It lasted for hours one Tuesday night, vibrating the floorboards in the hall.

David pressed his ear to their bedroom door, face pale. "It's... shifting things. Pushing against the walls.

Sarah gripped his arm. "It can't get out. The door's strong. The lock…"

"The lock is just brass," David whispered. "It's always just been the rules keeping it in."

The next Friday, the bowl of meat scraps was untouched by morning, a first. That night, the low gurgling sounds changed. They became sharper, frustrated, angry. A rhythmic *bang...bang....bang* vibrated up through the wall. They could feel the vibration in their chests as they lay in bed.

"It's hitting the walls," Ethan said at breakfast. His eyes were hollow. "It's getting harder."

Lily wouldn't go downstairs alone anymore.

The smell worsened. The dampness soured, mixing with a sharp, putrid tang like spoiled meat left in the sun. It leaked out from under its room door, staining the air in the hall.

Then, the door rattled. Not a random vibration. A deliberate, testing *jiggle* of the handle, once, twice. Late on a Sunday night, David stood frozen in the hallway, a glass of water forgotten in his hand, watching the brass knob twist slightly back and forth. The lock held, this time. The rattling stopped, replaced by a low, vibrating hiss that seemed to emanate from within the wood itself.

Grandpa Joe, who lived in the converted attic and remembered the house before the Millers, came down the next morning. His face was grave. He rarely spoke of the room under the stairs. Now, he stood before its door, a tremor in his wrinkled hands.

"It's cramped," he stated, his voice rough. "Always was. But it was...content. For a while. It liked the dark. The closeness. Not anymore." He turned to David and Sarah, his eyes fearful. "It feels the space above. The space beyond. It *wants* it. The whole house."

Sarah felt cold. "It can't have it. This is our home."

Grandpa Joe shook his head slowly. "It doesn't care. It grows. It hungers for more than meat scraps now. It hungers for...room. For space." He stepped closer to the door, leaning his ear against the weathered wood. He listened for a long moment, then jerked back as if burned. His face lost all color. "It knows we're here. It knows we're afraid. It's tired of the dark."

He vanished that night. They found his bed empty. The attic window was locked from the inside. The only trace was a single, muddy footprint just outside the door to the room under the stairs – too large, misshapen, with deep claw marks gouged into the wood floor beside it. The footprint pointed *out* into the hall.

Panic, cold and sharp, replaced their usual resigned dread. The rules were failing. The thing was testing its cage. Grandpa Joe was gone. The untouched meat scraps confirmed a terrifying shift: the under-stairs diet was no longer sufficient.

Three nights after Grandpa Joe vanished, the power went out. Not the whole street, just their house. The sudden plunge into absolute darkness was suffocating. The family huddled together in the living room, a single flickering candle casting monstrous, dancing shadows.

Silence. Thick, heavy silence. Then, a new sound. Not from under the stairs, from the *kitchen*. It was a wet, dragging shuffle. The scrape of something heavy moving across linoleum. The clatter of a pot falling from the drying rack.

David stood up slowly, the baseball bat he kept by the couch gripped tight. "Stay here," he whispered.

He edged towards the kitchen doorway, the candle flame trembling in his hand. The shuffling sound stopped. David peered around the doorframe.

The candlelight spilled into the kitchen, illuminating the edge of the table, the counter...and a shadow that didn't belong. Thick, dark, and glistening wetly, it pooled on the floor near the sink. It wasn't just a shadow. It had *substance*. Tendrils of darkness seemed to writhe at its edges. The smell hit him – that putrid, earthy stench, concentrated, overwhelming. It came from the shadow.

It wasn't in the room under the stairs. It was *in* the kitchen. It had gotten out.

David froze. The shadow pulsed, slowly, deliberately. It began to slide forward across the floor, towards the living room doorway. Towards his family.

He slammed the kitchen door shut. "Sarah! Kids! Upstairs! NOW!"

He braced his back against the door. Immediately, a massive force slammed into it from the other side. The solid wood groaned. The hinges squeaked. David dug his heels in, the baseball bat forgotten. The force came again and again. Not a ramming, a slow, relentless *pushing*. The door bulged inward then splintered near the lock.

Sarah screamed, grabbing the children and dragging them towards the stairs. Ethan stumbled, looking back in terror at the buckling kitchen door.

"DAVID!"

"GO!" he roared, bracing harder. The pushing stopped. Silence. Then, a different sound. A soft, tearing sound, like the ripping of canvas, coming from the base of the door. David looked down.

Darkness was seeping under the door. Not a shadow, a thick, tar-like substance, cold and smelling of the grave. It flowed across the floorboards towards his feet, he jerked back. The substance gathered, coalescing, rising from the floor. It formed a thick, trunk-like appendage, ending in three hooked, glistening claws. It scraped against the door, testing.

David swung the bat. It passed through the appendage like smoke, meeting no resistance, throwing him off balance. The claws lashed out, swift as a snake. They didn't tear flesh. They passed *into* David's chest. He felt no pain. Only an instant, soul-crushing coldness that spread from the point of contact, freezing his breath, locking his muscles. He couldn't move, couldn't scream. He saw the darkness flowing *up* the claw, into his body. The candle dropped from his numb hand, sputtering out.

Sarah watched from the stairs, frozen in horror. She saw her husband stiffen, his eyes wide and unseeing in the sudden gloom. She saw the dark appendage withdraw, pulling something shimmering and faintly luminous from David's chest back under the door. David collapsed like a puppet with cut strings.

The relentless pushing on the kitchen door resumed, harder now. The wood around the lock splintered even more with a sharp crack.

Sarah didn't scream. A terrible calm descended. The rules were over, the room under the stairs was empty. The monstrosity had chosen its new home, the whole house.

She grabbed Lily and Ethan, pulling them not upstairs, but towards the front door. It was locked, bolted. She fumbled with the chain. She was too slow.

The kitchen door exploded inward, not with a crash, but a deep, tearing sigh. Darkness flowed into the hallway, not as a shape, but an *absence* of light, a living void that drank the faint moonlight from the hall window. It pulsated with a deep, internal rhythm. It radiated cold and that suffocating stench. It filled the hallway, blocking their escape.

It moved towards them, slowly, deliberately. The temperature plummeted. Lily whimpered. Ethan stared, paralyzed.

Sarah backed them towards the only place left: the room under the stairs. The door hung open, the interior a world of pure blackness. The space seemed larger now, hungry.

The living darkness filled the hall, pressing closer. It didn't rush, it had all the time in the world. Its new home was almost ready.

Sarah made a decision. A terrible, final decision born of twelve years of fear and the instinct to survive. She yanked open the room's door wider. She pushed Ethan and Lily towards the opening.

"Inside! Quick! It's the only place it *isn't*!"

The children hesitated, staring into the suffocating blackness they'd feared their whole lives.

"NOW!" Sarah screamed, shoving them in. She followed, scrambling into the cramped, stinking space, pulling the door shut behind them with a slam. She fumbled in the dark, finding the old, heavy bolt inside and slamming it closed. They huddled together, breathing in the stale, terrifying air, listening.

Silence from the room under he stairs but outside the thin wooden door, in the hall, the house creaked. Floorboards groaned under immense, unseen weight. The wet, dragging shuffle moved past their hiding place, heading towards the stairs. Towards the bedrooms, towards the rest of its domain.

They were safe, for now. Trapped in the dark, cramped prison the monstrosity had rejected. They heard the heavy tread moving above them. It was exploring, claiming, settling into its spacious new home. The house belonged to it now. The Millers were the ones under the stairs. Listening, waiting, knowing the bolt on their door felt flimsy. Knowing the thing outside had grown too big for its old home, and the entire house might still be too small for its hunger. The room under the stairs was dark and quiet. The air was stale and hard to breathe. The scratching started on the other side of the room's door. It was gentle, patient, curious. The children clutched Sarah, their small bodies shaking. The new rules were just beginning.

The Man Who Loved the Rain

Rain hammered Cedar Point. It fell in thick sheets, turning streets into rivers, drumming a relentless rhythm on roofs. Most people huddled inside, cursing the gray skies. But not him.

They called him the Man Who Loved the Rain. No one knew his real name. He lived on the outskirts, in a house perpetually shrouded by dripping trees. He appeared only during storms. He was tall, thin, wrapped in a long, dark coat that never seemed truly wet, just slick. He walked the empty streets, face upturned, a faint smile as the water streamed down his skin. He moved slowly, deliberately, a dark figure against the downpour.

And people died when he walked.

It started small. Old Mrs. Arbogast slipped on her porch steps during a sudden gust of wind. A tragic accident, they said. But her neighbor swore she saw the tall man standing at the end of the path just before, motionless in the rain.

Then there was Tom Henderson. He went out to secure his boat during a gale. He was found the next morning, drowned in three feet of water near the dock. His face held an expression of pure terror, not the blank shock of accidental drowning. The storm surge hadn't reached that spot. Rain splashed the scene. A fisherman reported seeing the tall man near the marina hours before.

Fear began to spread through Cedar Point. It wasn't fear of the storms, but of the dark figure who welcomed them. People whispered stories of the Man Who Loved the Rain. He became a local legend. The more the stories were told, the more absurd they became.

Sheriff Dale Miller felt the weight of it. He was a practical man. He believed in evidence, in chains of cause and effect. Accidents happened. People took risks in bad weather. Coincidence explained the man's presence. But the whispers grew louder, the patterns harder to ignore.

"Always when it rains hard, Sheriff," Mrs. Phelps insisted, her knuckles white on her umbrella handle after young Billy Carson vanished. Billy had run out to fetch his dog during a thunderstorm. The dog returned, whimpering. Billy did not. A search found nothing. Then, two days later, after another downpour, his small body washed up near the old mill. The water level shouldn't have carried him there. The rain had been fierce that night. And a deputy, checking the mill perimeter earlier, swore he glimpsed a tall figure standing silently beneath the leaking eaves.

Sheriff Miller increased patrols during storms. He questioned the Man Who Loved the Rain once. The man answered politely, vaguely. He liked the rain, yes. Found it peaceful. Cleansing. He walked to feel it. He had seen nothing unusual near the marina, or the mill, or Mrs. Arbogast's house. His pale eyes, the color of rain-heavy clouds, held no malice, only a deep, unsettling calm. Sheriff Miller found no reason to hold him. No evidence linked him to anything but walking in the wet.

The deaths continued.

A transformer blew during a violent electrical storm, plunging Elm Street into darkness. Frank Reynolds, heading home from the late shift, took a shortcut through the pitch-black alley behind the diner. His body was found the next morning. Not electrocuted. Not robbed. His neck was broken. The alley floor was slick with rain. Footprints, large and deep, led away from the body and vanished at the alley's mouth, as if the walker had simply dissolved into the downpour. A diner cook, peering out the back door during the blackout, reported seeing a tall shape standing motionless at the far end of the alley just before the lights died.

Cedar Creek swelled over its banks after days of torrential rain. The Evans family tried to evacuate their farmhouse too late. Their truck stalled in rising water. Rescuers found the parents clinging to a tree downstream. Their teenage daughter, Sarah, was missing. Search teams battled the current. Then, as the rain finally eased to a drizzle, her body was discovered wedged under a bridge piling upstream from where the truck stalled. An impossible location unless carried *against* the current. A farmer checking his flooded fields miles upstream claimed he saw a tall man standing knee-deep in the raging creek water the night Sarah vanished, just staring into the flood. He dismissed it as stress, until he heard about the body's location.

Panic set in. People locked their doors tight when the clouds gathered. They drew curtains. They listened to the drumming rain with dread. The Man Who Loved the Rain still walked. His smile seemed wider now, his pale eyes brighter in the gloom. He became a shadow glimpsed between sheets of rain, a figure standing too still at the edge of a sodden field, a dark presence felt just beyond the circle of porch light.

Sheriff Miller stopped believing in coincidence. He started watching the man's house. It stood silent, windows dark even during the day, surrounded by dripping pines. No car. No visitors. Sheriff Miller never saw the man leave except when the rain fell hard. He never saw him return.

The storm that hit Cedar Point two weeks after Sarah Evans' funeral wasn't just rain. It was a deluge. The sky opened, unleashing a waterfall that blurred the world. Thunder shook houses. Lightning ripped the sky white, freezing the lashing rain in jagged streaks. Power died across town.

Sheriff Miller was out in it, radio crackling with static, responding to reports of downed trees. His headlights carved weak tunnels through the solid wall of water. He rounded a bend near the old cemetery. His beams swept across the road, illuminating a figure.

The Man Who Loved the Rain.

He stood in the center of the road, coat plastered dark against his thin frame, face lifted to the punishing sky. He wasn't smiling. His expression was rapturous, intense. Rain streamed down his face like tears, but his eyes were open, drinking it in.

Sheriff Miller slammed the brakes. The cruiser skidded on the slick asphalt, stopping mere feet from the man. The man didn't flinch. He slowly lowered his head. Those pale eyes locked onto the Sheriff's through the rain-streaked windshield. They held no fear, only a chilling intensity, a deep, alien connection to the chaos around them.

Sheriff Miller grabbed his heavy flashlight, heart pounding in his chest. He threw the car door open, the roar of the rain instantly swallowing the sound. He stepped out into the maelstrom. Water instantly soaked him to the skin, cold and shocking.

"Hey!" Sheriff Miller shouted, his voice torn away by the wind. He raised the flashlight beam, illuminating the man's face. "What are you doing out here?"

The man didn't answer immediately. He blinked slowly, water dripping from his lashes. "Listening," he said, his voice unnaturally clear, cutting through the storm's roar. "Feeling it. It sings tonight."

"It's dangerous!" Sheriff Miller yelled, hand instinctively near his holster. "Get off the road! People get hurt in weather like this!"

The man tilted his head. A ghost of that familiar, unsettling smile spread crookedly across his lips. "Hurt? Sometimes. Sometimes...it needs feeding." His gaze drifted past the Sheriff, towards the town lights struggling through the downpour. "It gets hungry. So hungry."

Ice shot through Sheriff Miller's veins. "Feeding? What needs feeding?" He took a step closer, flashlight beam steady on the man's face. Rain stung his own eyes.

The man looked back at him, his pale eyes seeming to glow faintly in the flashlight's beam. "The rain, Sheriff. The storm. It lives. It hungers. Not for water." He raised a hand, palm up, catching the torrent. "For life. For the spark. The fear. The final gasp." He closed his fingers slowly, as if crushing something fragile. "It needs...endings."

Sheriff Miller's blood ran cold. The absurdity warred with the chilling certainty in the man's voice, the pattern of deaths echoing in his mind. "You're talking nonsense! Did you hurt those people? Billy Carson? Sarah Evans?"

The man's smile widened, showing teeth. "Hurt? I am the conduit. The vessel it chooses. I walk where it falls hardest. I feel its hunger. I...draw it to where the spark is brightest. The fearful. The reckless. The lonely." He took a step towards the Sheriff, unbothered by the cruiser's proximity. "Like young Billy, running scared for his dog. Like Sarah, trapped and terrified in the rising dark. Like..." His eyes flickered past the Sheriff again, towards the flooded creek road. "...like the man in the blue truck, stuck in the water just past Tully's Bend."

Sheriff Miller froze. He hadn't heard any call about a truck at Tully's Bend. His radio had been dead static for minutes. A fresh wave of terror washed over him, colder than the rain. "What man?"

The Man Who Loved the Rain ignored him. He closed his eyes, inhaling deeply, as if savoring a fine wine. "Ah. There. The spark flickers. Bright. Afraid. Alone." He opened his eyes, fixing the Sheriff with that unnerving gaze. "It's time. The storm demands its due."

He turned and began walking down the center of the road, away from the Sheriff, towards Tully's Bend. Not hurrying. A deliberate, steady pace, merging with the downpour.

"Stop!" Sheriff Miller yelled, drawing his service weapon. The rain made the grip slick. "Stop right there!"

The man didn't pause. He didn't look back.

Sheriff Miller hesitated only a second. The image of another body found after the rain, another family shattered, flashed in his mind. He couldn't let the man reach that bend. He leveled his weapon. "I said STOP! Hands where I can see them!"

The man kept walking. Twenty yards. Fifteen.

Sheriff Miller fired a warning shot into the air. The crack was swallowed instantly by thunder. The man didn't flinch. Ten yards.

Sheriff Miller sighted on the man's leg. He squeezed the trigger.

The gunshot was loud, sharp. The man staggered. He stopped. Slowly, he turned. Rain plastered his hair to his skull. He looked down at his leg. Dark bloomed on the wet fabric of his trousers, spreading rapidly, diluted by the rain. He looked up at the Sheriff. There was no pain in his face. Only surprise. Then, a deeper, colder expression. Betrayal? Anger? Something ancient and inhuman.

He took a limping step back towards the Sheriff. Then another. His movements were jerky now, but his eyes never left the Sheriff's. That chilling intensity burned brighter.

The Sheriff braced himself, finger tightening on the trigger for a second shot. "Down on the ground! NOW!"

The man was five yards away. He stopped. He raised his hand, not in surrender, but palm out towards the Sheriff. The rain seemed to intensify around him, forming a shimmering curtain.

"It wasn't my time, Sheriff," the man said, his voice suddenly thick, strained. Blood mingled with rainwater at his feet. "But the storm...it won't be denied its meal. It needs an ending."

He swayed. The pale light in his eyes flickered, dimmed. He looked down at his bleeding leg again, confusion replacing the intensity. He took a shuddering breath. "I...I just loved the rain..." His voice was a whisper, lost in the downpour. He took one more faltering step forward.

Then his legs buckled. He crumpled to the slick asphalt, landing heavily on his side. He didn't move. The dark stain around his leg widened, a macabre flower blooming in the rushing water on the road.

Sheriff Miller stood frozen, gun still raised, heart pounding like a drum against his ribs. Rain hammered his face, blurring his vision. He waited, tense, expecting...something. A trick. A final surge. The man lay still, too still.

Slowly, cautiously, the Sheriff approached, flashlight beam fixed on the prone figure. He kicked the man's outstretched hand. No reaction. He knelt, keeping his distance, and felt for a pulse at the neck. Nothing. Cold skin. Lifeless.

Relief, cold and shaky, washed over him. It was over. The nightmare of Cedar Point. He'd stopped him. He'd had to. The man had confessed. He'd been heading towards another victim.

The Sheriff holstered his weapon, his hands trembling slightly. He needed to call it in. Report the shooting. Secure the scene. He stood, turning back towards his cruiser, fumbling for the radio mic inside.

The roar of the rain was the only sound. The radio hissed dead static. The Sheriff clicked the transmit button. "Dispatch, this is Unit One. Shots fired. Suspect down. Requesting backup and medical at my location, near the cemetery on Old Mill Road. Suspect is..." He paused, looking back at the body lying in the road. "...the Man Who Loved the Rain. He's deceased."

He released the button. Only static answered. He tried again. "Dispatch, Unit One, do you copy?" Nothing. The storm must have knocked out the repeater. He'd have to drive to the station.

He turned back towards the cruiser. The headlights still cut through the rain, illuminating the empty road where the man had fallen.

The road was empty.

Sheriff Miller took a breath. He swept the flashlight beam frantically across the asphalt. Nothing. Only rushing water, reflecting the cruiser's lights. No body. No dark stain. Just rain and wet pavement.

Impossible. He'd felt the lack of pulse. Seen the blood. He'd only turned his back for seconds.

A sound made him whirl around. A low, wet gurgle. It came from the ditch beside the road. The sheriff pointed the flashlight.

The man lay half-submerged in the muddy, fast-flowing runoff. His eyes were open, staring blankly at the raging sky. Rain filled his open mouth. His coat snagged on a submerged branch. Water surged over his chest. His face was pale, waxy. Utterly dead.

The sheriff scrambled down the slippery bank, flashlight beam jerking. He reached the edge of the ditch. The water was rising rapidly, fed by the torrential downpour. It tugged at the man's body. Sheriff Miller leaned down, grabbing the collar of the coat, trying to pull him free of the branch. The body was heavy, waterlogged. The mud sucked at the sheriff's boots.

With a sickening tear, the coat ripped. The body surged forward with the current, pulled free by the force of the water. It rolled once, face down, and was swept away into the darkness downstream, vanishing into the curtain of rain.

Sheriff Miller stood knee-deep in the icy runoff, clutching a torn piece of dark fabric, staring into the blackness where the body had disappeared. Shock numbed him. The storm roared around him. He needed to pursue. He needed to recover the body. He needed proof.

He slogged back up the bank to his cruiser. He got in, dripping water onto the seat, and slammed it into gear. He drove slowly down Old Mill Road, following the ditch line, high beams piercing the rain, scanning the rushing brown water. Nothing. He reached Tully's Bend. The creek had overflowed its banks, turning the low-lying road into a shallow, fast-moving river. A blue pickup truck was stranded, water up to its doors. A man stood on the roof, waving frantically, screaming soundlessly against the storm.

Sheriff Miller radioed again, uselessly. He activated his light bar, hoping to signal the man he was seen. He'd need the fire department's boat for this. He stopped the cruiser a safe distance back, putting on his emergency brake. He grabbed a life vest and a rope from the trunk.

As he turned back towards the stranded truck, something made him look upstream. The ditch he'd followed fed into the flooded creek right here. The water churned brown and violent.

A dark shape tumbled in the current near the confluence. It rolled sluggishly. For a moment, caught in the cruiser's high beams, it surfaced. Pale face. Open mouth filled with water. Sightless eyes reflecting the red and blue emergency lights. The Man Who Loved the Rain.

Then the current grabbed the body, pulling it under the surface near the truck's submerged front end. The man on the truck's roof stopped waving. He stared down into the water directly in front of him, his face contorted in new terror. He pointed, screaming.

The sheriff started wading towards the truck, rope ready, eyes fixed on the spot where the body had vanished. He saw nothing but churning water.

A hand broke the surface near the truck's grille. Not reaching for help. Pale. Lifeless. It slapped against the hood with a wet thud, fingers splayed. Then it was gone, pulled under the vehicle.

The man on the roof screamed again, a raw sound of pure horror. He scrambled backwards on the wet metal.

Sheriff Miller pushed forward, the water now waist-deep and pulling hard. "Hold on! I'm coming!" His voice was lost.

He reached the driver's side door. The window was open. Water surged inside. He hooked the rope to the door frame. "Grab the rope!" he yelled up at the man on the roof.

The man didn't move. He stared down into the water beside the truck, transfixed, shaking his head violently. "Under...it's under...!" he shrieked.

The sheriff looked down. The churning water was thick with mud. He saw nothing. He threw the end of the rope up onto the roof. "Grab it! Now! Tie it off!"

The man finally moved, fumbling for the rope with trembling hands. He looped it around his waist.

A surge of water hit the truck, rocking it violently. The man on the roof lost his balance. He fell sideways with a cry, plunging into the rushing water beside the cab. He surfaced instantly, sputtering, grabbed the rope, and was swept downstream, held only by the line attached to the truck.

"Hold on!" Sheriff Miller bellowed, bracing himself against the current, ready to pull the man back hand-over-hand once he stopped being dragged.

The man floundered, fighting the current, his head barely above water. Suddenly, his eyes widened in unimaginable terror. He screamed, a gurgling, choked sound. He was pulled sharply *downward*, as if something massive had grabbed his legs from below. His head vanished under the brown water. The rope snapped tight.

Sheriff Miller pulled with all his strength. The rope resisted, then went suddenly slack. Too slack. It slithered back through the flooded ditch towards him, limp and empty.

He stared at the loose end of the rope in his hand, then at the spot where the man had disappeared. Only churning water. No sign of him. No sign of the pale body.

The rain beat down. The storm raged. The red and blue lights of the cruiser reflected on the rushing water, painting the scene in ghastly hues. Sheriff Miller stood alone in the flood, the roar of the rain the only sound, the torn piece of dark coat still clutched in his other hand. He looked at it. Just fabric. Wet. Cold.

He looked back at the empty rope. The empty water.

He understood.

He hadn't stopped anything. He hadn't killed the Man Who Loved the Rain. He had fed the storm. He had given it an ending – the man's ending. And the storm, furious, denied its intended meal at Tully's Bend, had taken another. It had taken the man from the truck. It had taken payment.

The rain drummed on the sheriff's head, his shoulders. It felt different now. Not just water. It felt watchful. Hungry. He looked up into the black, pouring sky. He thought he saw, for a fleeting second in a lightning flash, a tall, thin outline against the clouds, arms outstretched. Then darkness swallowed it.

The Man Who Loved the Rain was gone. But the rain remained. And Sheriff Miller knew, with a certainty colder than the floodwater around his legs, that it would walk again. It would find new fear. It would demand new endings. Cedar Point's nightmare wasn't over. It had just changed shape. It was the rain itself. And it was always hungry.

The Breathing

The house was quiet when the voice came from the stairs.

"Can you hear it breathing? I can."

Joe and Erica froze. Their daughter, Emily, stood at the bottom of the steps in her pajamas, her small fingers gripping the railing. Her eyes were wide, fixed on the ceiling.

Erica set down her coffee. "Hear what, sweetheart?"

Emily didn't blink. "Upstairs. In my room."

Joe forced a laugh. "Probably just the wind, kiddo."

Emily shook her head. "No. It's loud. Like this." She sucked in a sharp breath, held it, then let it out in a slow, wet rasp.

Erica's skin tingled.

They checked the room. Nothing. The window was shut. The closet empty. Joe patted Emily's head. "See? Nothing to worry about."

Emily stared at the corner of the room. "It stopped when you came in."

That night, Erica woke to a sound—a deep, rhythmic exhale, just beyond the door. She shook Joe awake.

"Listen."

Silence.

Then it came again. A breath, too slow, too heavy.

Joe grabbed the baseball bat from under the bed. He swung the door open.

The hallway was empty.

The next morning, Emily didn't come down for breakfast. Erica called up the stairs. There was no answer.

She found Emily sitting on her bed, facing the wall.

"It talks now," Emily said.

Erica's mouth went dry. "What did it say?"

Emily turned. Her pupils were too wide, her voice flat. "It wants me to go with it."

Joe tore the house apart. He checked the attic, the vents, the crawl space. He found nothing.

That night, they locked Emily's door from the outside.

Eric woke to the sound of scratching. Something dragged across the other side of the door, slow and deliberate.

Then Emily's voice came through the wood.

"Mom. It's in here with me."

Erica fumbled with the lock. Joe shoved the door open.

The room was cold. Emily sat on the bed, her back to them.

"Emily?" Erica reached for her.

Emily turned.

Her mouth stretched too wide. Her breath came out in that same wet rasp.

Then she spoke—but not in her own voice.

"You should have listened."

The door slammed shut behind them. The neighbors called the police when the screaming started. By the time they broke in, the house was silent.

They found Joe and Erica in Emily's room. Their faces were frozen in terror. Their chests didn't move. Emily was gone. Upstairs, the window was open. From the woods beyond the house, something breathed.

Final Frame

Elise rented the apartment on a Sunday afternoon. The ad said top floor, good light, long windows. She didn't ask about the price. She didn't ask about the history. She just needed a place alone. The landlord gave her one rule: don't touch the painting.

The hallway leading to the apartment was narrow and silent. The door opened into a wide living space with polished black floors and red walls. It was empty except for a large painting hanging across from the window. A woman in a black dress. She stood with one arm across her waist, the other at her side, her head turned slightly as if she'd just been spoken to.

Elise didn't ask who she was.

She didn't care.

That first night, the shadows from the window cut sharp lines across the floor. The moonlight turned the red walls dark. Elise made a bed on the floor. She didn't sleep much. She kept looking at the painting.

In the morning, the woman in the painting had shifted. Her arm rested against her hip now. Elise told herself she was wrong. Memory plays tricks. Light changes things.

She made coffee. No TV. No internet. She liked it that way. Quiet. Clean. Still.

That night, the woman in the painting faced forward. Elise sat in the hallway, staring through the open door. She didn't go inside. She didn't sleep. The next morning, the painting was normal again. Or maybe not. The woman's eyes looked brighter. The mouth had parted.

Elise started leaving the lights on.

On the third night, she stepped inside to get her jacket. She felt watched. Not just by the painting. The room itself felt aware.

She turned to leave and the painting whispered.

Not words. Just sound. Breath moving against canvas.

Elise didn't go back for her jacket.

The next day she covered the painting with a sheet. The fabric stuck to the surface. It didn't fall. It clung like skin.

That night, the sheet was gone. Folded neatly on the floor.

The woman in the painting now faced the door. Eyes fixed on it. Elise stood at the threshold. She didn't step inside. The air felt wrong. Too warm, too still.

She closed the door and locked it. It didn't help. At 3:12 a.m., the door opened by itself. Elise woke on the hallway floor.

The painting had changed again. Now the woman stood closer to the edge of the frame. Her eyes stared down the hall.

Elise ran.

She spent the next night in the stairwell. The lights above her buzzed faintly. She didn't sleep.

In the morning, the landlord was waiting at her door. He smiled. No questions. Just a reminder. Don't touch the painting.

She hadn't touched it. She told him that. He looked past her into the room and walked away.

She shut the door. The woman in the painting now stood in the center, closer, larger.

Her eyes followed Elise.

Elise moved her sleeping spot to the kitchen. No windows, no shadows. She kept the door to the main room shut. She pushed a chair under the knob.

It didn't matter.

Each morning the door was open. Each morning the painting had changed.

The woman now pressed both hands against the inside of the canvas. Her face stretched, not screaming—pressing—like glass between her and Elise.

Elise found deep scratches on the floorboards leading from the painting to the hallway.

111

That night, she stayed in the bathroom, she locked the door, she held a knife. At 3:12, she heard footsteps, slow, across the hall. The doorknob didn't turn. But something scraped against the door, a hand, or nails. She didn't open it.

When she did—at dawn—nothing waited for her, except a new painting in the hall. It was the same woman, standing outside a red door. It was Elise's door.

She left the apartment that afternoon. She booked a motel.

Two days passed, then the photo arrived. There was no return address. Just a single Polaroid. It was her motel room, taken from inside.

She packed and ran. She didn't go home, she didn't return to the city. She found a small town and paid cash for a cabin.

No address. No mailbox. No neighbors.

She thought she was safe. On the seventh night, she saw her, not in a painting. In the window, a reflection, the same black dress. She turned around. There was nothing there.

She boarded the windows. She smashed every mirror.

The next morning, the painting leaned against the cabin wall. The woman closer still. Only her shoulder and one eye visible now. Elise burned it. She watched the fire eat through the frame, curl the canvas, blacken the image. She stood in the ashes, the eye still stared up at her, unburned. She buried it in the woods.

That night, the bed was soaked. A voice whispered behind her ear. She didn't turn around. The next morning, the painting hung above the bed. Whole again. Now the woman stood outside a cabin door, Elise's door. She nailed the frame to the wall, it bled. The wood ran dark and sticky.

She didn't eat for days, didn't sleep. She stopped looking at the painting. She couldn't move it, couldn't cover it. It moved on its own, it followed her from room to room. She opened the cabin door to leave. Behind it: the painting. Now showing a bedroom. Her bedroom, empty. She slammed the door and locked it. Behind her, the woman stood in the hallway. Not in paint, not in canvas, she was in the house.

112

The dress dripped. The face was like wet paint. She moved without sound. Elise ran. She made it to the basement, locked the door. She heard footsteps. Then nothing, only silence. She stayed there for hours. When she came out, the woman was gone. So was the painting.

The cabin stood empty, except for a mirror. One she hadn't seen before. It hung in the hall where the painting used to be. She stepped in front of it. It didn't show her. It showed the room behind her. The woman standing there, smiling. Then it showed nothing.

Now she's inside. Not the cabin, the frame. She watches from the glass, eyes wide, mouth open—waiting. The apartment is empty again. The painting has returned. The woman wears Elise's face now. And she looks at you. From the frame.

The Face in the Fog

No one saw where the fog came from. It wasn't in the forecast. It didn't roll in from the coast or rise off the river. It just appeared, thick and heavy. It swallowed the neighborhood in less than an hour.

Alex stood at the window of his apartment, watching the street vanish. His phone buzzed with alerts—visibility warnings, road closures, power fluctuations. A voice on the emergency channel advised residents to stay indoors until further notice.

By noon, the sun was gone. The fog turned darker. It pressed against the windows like smoke.

Alex tried calling his brother. No signal. No data. Every app failed to load. He turned on the TV. It was all static, then black.

Something moved past the window.

He leaned closer. It was just a blur, it didn't walk, it drifted.

He stepped back and shut the blinds. The walls felt closer than usual. The silence pressed into his head.

His phone vibrated again. One new voicemail. The caller ID was blank. He pressed play.

At first, there was only static. Then came a long, low sound. Like a moan. It was a low screech, rising to a scream. Alex dropped the phone. The sound didn't stop. It kept pouring from the speaker until the screen cracked.

He backed away.

Then the lights went out.

The room was silent again, too silent. He heard no traffic, no wind. Not even his own heartbeat. He tried to call out, but his voice sounded wrong, flat, muffled.

The fog crept under the front door. Thick tendrils slid across the floor, climbing the furniture, reaching for the ceiling. They formed slow circles, as if searching.

Alex grabbed a flashlight and turned it on. The beam barely cut through the haze.

He opened a window to try to vent it. Cold air poured in, but so did more fog. It flooded the room and swirled fast.

He slammed the window shut.

The fog moved with purpose now. It drew together in the middle of the room, folding inward, shaping itself.

A face emerged.

Eyes like pits. Nose sharp. Mouth wide open, stretching wider.

The room shook with a low, hollow sound.

The face in the fog screamed. The sound came from everywhere— walls, floor, ceiling. It wasn't loud, it was deep, felt more than heard. It vibrated in his ribs and behind his eyes.

He ran.

The hallway was filled with it too. The same shape forming in the air—face, mouth, screaming silently.

Apartment doors stood open. Lights flickered and went dark. One door hung crooked on its hinges. Inside, a chair rocked slowly with no one in it. He ran down the stairs two at a time.

The lobby was filled with fog. There was no front desk, no exit. Just the face, again and again, floating in the haze. Each mouth wider than the last. Each scream silent but suffocating.

He forced the emergency door open and ran outside.

The street was unrecognizable. Every car sat empty, doors open, engines dead. Streetlights flashed, then failed. Shapes moved through the fog. Some walked, some crawled, none had eyes.

He ran until he couldn't breathe. Then he saw the building. His brother's apartment. The lobby door stood open. He rushed inside, calling out. There was only silence.

He climbed the stairs. The air grew heavier, each breath stung, his eyes burned.

His brother's door was ajar. He pushed it open. The fog sat in the center of the room. It was thick, unmoving. A shape stood within it, tall, still.

"Matt?" he called.

There was no answer.

He stepped forward. The fog shifted, and the shape turned. It wasn't his brother.

The thing wore his face, but it was stretched, hollow, tight skin. The mouth opened too wide. Inside was only more blackness.

It stepped toward him.

Alex backed into the hall, heart racing. He turned to run, but the fog behind him was alive. Dozens of faces formed, all open-mouthed, all screaming.

He tried to scream back but nothing came out.

The faces closed in, the mouths opened wider. He fell backward into the room, crawling until he hit the far wall. The light overhead flickered once and died.

Then silence—Not just quiet but an absence of sound. He couldn't feel the floor anymore, couldn't feel his body. He opened his mouth to cry out. The fog poured in. It filled his throat, lungs, eyes. It didn't suffocate him. It erased him. He became part of it.

The next morning, the fog lifted. Emergency responders searched the area. They found no bodies, no blood, no signs of life. Every building stood intact, lights still on, doors still open. But inside each room, the walls whispered. And the mirrors didn't reflect what stood in front of them.

She Who Waits by the Water

They said the lake was cursed. No official records, no news reports, just warnings passed down in quiet voices by old locals. The stories always centered around a woman. Sometimes she danced, sometimes she floated but she always appeared at dusk. Always near the flat rocks by the water's edge. Always alone.

David didn't believe in curses. He came to the woods to photograph something real. The landscape was untouched, the lake still. He parked on the gravel road and hiked through the underbrush, his camera slung over his shoulder. It was his third visit. The first two, he'd captured fog moving low over the water. The third, he wanted something better, something with presence.

At the edge of the lake, the rocks stretched out into the water like a natural platform. The trees stood thick behind him, no paths, no markers, just silence. He set up his tripod and waited. The sun lowered behind the trees, casting long shadows. He took a few shots of the still lake, the distant hills, the rippling surface. Then he saw her.

She stepped onto the rocks from somewhere he hadn't seen. She was tall, barefoot, wrapped in gauze-like fabric that moved with the breeze. Her arms lifted, cloth stretched between them like wings. Her face was pale, her eyes fixed forward.

David raised his camera. She didn't look at him. She didn't flinch at the sound of the shutter. She moved like she was in a trance. Her feet never stumbled. Her body swayed as if pulled by a rhythm only she could hear.

He called out, she didn't respond. He stepped closer. She held her position, arms out, fabric suspended. He circled the edge, snapping frame after frame. Her skin caught the light in a way that made her glow against the forest behind her.

Then she moved, not a turn, not a step. She floated, her feet stayed inches above the stone. The fabric around her lifted, even though the wind had stopped. David froze. She looked at him. He lowered the camera.

She smiled. It wasn't a warm smile. The folds of her robe peeled back. Inside was nothing, a hollow space, black, depthless. He stepped back. She moved forward, no sound, no weight. The rocks under her cracked.

He turned to run but the forest behind him had changed. There was no trail, no underbrush, just darkness. Trees too close together. Air too still. He turned again. She stood inches away. She placed her hand on his chest.

Cold spread from her fingers. His limbs stiffened. His knees buckled. He dropped to the stone, gasping, unable to breathe. She leaned close and whispered something he couldn't hear. His heart slowed. His eyes rolled back. Then everything stopped.

The camera sat untouched on the tripod. The lens pointed at the rock. The woman was gone. The lake was calm. A week passed. A hiker found the camera. It had one photo left. The woman stood on the rock, arms out, face blank.

Behind her, another figure hovered, frozen mid-fall. David. His mouth wide, eyes shut, hands reaching for help that never came. The woman's smile stretched wider. Then the image blurred. And the file corrupted.

No one could recover it. No one found David's body. But on quiet nights, some say they see two figures dancing at the lake's edge. One draped in silk. The other suspended in silence, waiting.

The Pumpkin Light

Mallory didn't want to decorate for Halloween that year. The house was too quiet. Her daughter, Callie, had gone missing the October before, vanishing from the front yard during trick-or-treating. No one had seen anything. No leads, no suspects, no answers. Just the costume left on the porch steps and one small plastic pumpkin bucket with candy untouched.

But something strange happened the night before Halloween. A small jack-o'-lantern light appeared in her front yard. It wasn't hers. It stood in the planter next to the hosta she never watered, glowing orange with a crooked smile carved into its cheap plastic face. She bent to remove it, thinking maybe it was a prank, but something stopped her. The soil was undisturbed. The label on the stake was clean, new, fresh. She hadn't heard anyone approach. No footprints in the soil. Nothing.

She left it there.

At dusk, the light turned on by itself. Mallory stood at the window and watched it flicker. No other lights were on in the neighborhood. It wasn't plugged in. It had no switch. She checked it again, holding the cold plastic in her hand. It didn't feel like a solar light. No battery compartment. There were no wires, just a smiling face that pulsed with orange warmth as if something inside it breathed.

That night, she dreamed of Callie. Her daughter stood barefoot in the hostas, holding the same jack-o'-lantern light. Her mouth opened, but no sound came out. Mallory tried to run to her, but the air felt thick. The ground cracked. A hand reached from the soil and pulled Callie down.

Mallory woke up gasping. The window was open. The wind had blown in dried leaves and dirt. Her bed was soaked in sweat, but her feet were cold. She checked the yard. The pumpkin still sat there, glowing, brighter now.

On Halloween morning, she walked the perimeter of her yard. No sign of digging, no disturbed earth. The neighbors hadn't seen anything. She called the police, again. They brushed her off with the same line she'd heard for a year. "If there's no evidence of a crime, there's nothing we can do."

That night, children passed her house in groups. None came to the door. Mallory left the light off. No candy, no decorations, just the strange jack-o'-lantern glowing on its stake. Sometime after nine, the children stopped coming. The street emptied. Mallory sat on the couch, staring out the window. The pumpkin light seemed brighter than the streetlamps. It almost pulsed in a rhythm.

Then she heard a knock, soft, slow. She opened the door and saw nothing. There were no children, no footsteps, just the sound of wind. Then she noticed the hosta. The soil beneath the pumpkin light churned slowly. Something was pushing up from beneath.

She stepped outside, walked down to the planter, and watched. A pale fingertip broke the dirt. Then another. A hand emerged, covered in mud, followed by part of an arm. Mallory backed away. The pumpkin's face flickered, the carved grin widening. She didn't scream, she couldn't.

The hand clawed its way out, followed by a forearm, a shoulder, and then a face.

Callie's face.

Rotting.

Wet.

Eyes missing.

Hair matted with soil and blood.

Mallory fell to her knees. Her mouth moved but no sound came out. The figure stopped halfway out of the ground, head tilted as if it were listening. The jack-o'-lantern flared with a surge of orange light. The child's body twitched. Something else moved beneath the hosta leaves.

Another hand. This one larger with jagged fingers, long nails. It grabbed Callie's shoulder and dragged her down.

Mallory lunged forward and grabbed her daughter's wrist, but the skin tore under her fingers. More hands reached out. Some clawed at the soil, some held bones, some still had skin and fingernails. One gripped her ankle. She screamed, finally.

She pulled away, but it yanked hard, and she landed in the soil. Her knees sank. She reached for the porch. It was too far. Another hand grabbed her wrist, another her neck. The jack-o'-lantern flickered wildly. It pulsed with every pull.

She screamed again, this time louder, tearing her throat. She clawed at the dirt, at the hosta, at the base of the light. The jack-o'-lantern spun slowly on its stake. She looked up, and for a moment, the face on the plastic pumpkin moved. Its eyes narrowed.

The light shut off.

The yard went silent.

By the time anyone noticed Mallory missing, her house sat dark and quiet. The only sign was the hosta planter, its soil churned and blackened, with the jack-o'-lantern still staked in the center, glowing again.

The smile was wider now.

Another Halloween came.

The light turned on by itself.

And beneath it, the soil moved.

The Velvet Stage

The Velvet Stage stood silent at the corner of Margrave Street, its doors locked since 1931. Locals whispered about its final show, a night soaked in blood and missing bodies. The owner sealed the theater after that, left the curtains drawn, and vanished. No one had stepped inside since.

Grace found the photo while cataloging estate donations at the historical society. A black-and-white print. A woman stood barefoot before a painted backdrop, dressed in black lace. Her expression was vacant, her eyes fixed on something outside the frame. The edges of the photo were curled, and someone had scratched a word onto the back: "Velouria."

Grace didn't recognize the name. No record of her in the society's archives, no mention in the playbills. She became obsessed. Every night she searched. Old newspapers, police records, journals. She found nothing.

Then, late one night, she found a listing from 1931. A short blurb in the Margrave Herald:

"Final performance scheduled for March 18 at the Velvet Stage. Madame Velouria returns in a new act—unpublished, unnamed."

That night, Grace dreamed of the woman in the photo. She stood behind the theater's curtain, whispering something Grace couldn't hear. When she woke, her ears rang, her nose bled.

She went to the building the next day.

The lock was rusted but loose. She stepped inside with a flashlight and a recorder, dust coated everything. The seats sagged, the floor creaked. The red velvet curtains hung heavy over the stage. The painted backdrop was still there—men with dogs, women with baskets, horses and wagons in a forest. It looked exactly like the photo.

Grace walked behind the curtain. A faint sound ticked through the silence, like heels on wood. She turned. The photo lay on the center of the stage. She hadn't brought it. She picked it up, cold, damp.

Something moved in the backdrop. Just behind the trees.

Grace looked again. The painted figure of a hunter had turned. His eyes followed her. His arm was raised. The musket he held pointed at her chest.

She blinked.

He hadn't moved.

But the woman in the lace was no longer in the photo. The background was there, the curtain, the floor. But she was gone.

A breath passed behind Grace.

She turned and saw a woman standing in the center of the stage. She was pale, dressed in lace. Her hair curled, her expression empty.

Grace whispered, "Velouria."

The woman opened her mouth. Black smoke poured out. Her feet didn't touch the floor. Her fingers stretched too long. Her eyes sank in.

Grace ran for the door, but the seats had changed. No longer dusty, no longer torn. Figures filled them, dressed in suits and gowns from another century, all silent, all watching.

She climbed onto the stage. The backdrop shifted again. The painted people walked, slowly, toward her. Dogs sniffed. Horses pawed the ground. Their eyes gleamed with light.

Grace turned to run backstage but found only darkness. The floor gave way, she fell. When she landed, the world was flat, painted, stiff.

The trees around her didn't sway. The air didn't move. The forest was fake, but she couldn't leave.

She screamed, but no sound came. Behind her, Velouria walked toward her, one hand raised. The curtain closed. Outside, the building sat quiet. But now the woman in the photo had company. Grace stood beside Velouria.

Eyes empty.

Mouth closed.

Waiting.

The Witch of the Forest
Does Not Forget

The village of Briar's End huddled under a perpetual twilight. Sunlight never truly reached the cobbled streets; the towering, ancient forest pressed in like a neglected wall, its branches twisted into skeletal claws against the bruised sky. A curse held them. For generations, no one could leave. Stepping beyond the last thatched roof meant hitting an invisible, unyielding barrier, cold as the grave. Crops withered in the fields. Livestock sickened and died. Children whispered of the Crone, the Witch of the Deep Woods, who blamed them all for a sin committed centuries before their grandparents were born. Her vengeance was indiscriminate, eternal. Strange lights flickered in the forest depths at night. Unearthly howls carried on the wind, chilling the blood. Shadows moved where no one stood. Fear was in the air they breathed.

Old Man Finn discovered the crack. It happened near the crumbling stone well at the forest's very edge, furthest from the village square. He'd stumbled chasing a sickly chicken, his hand passing through the barrier for a single, heart-stopping moment. He pulled back, trembling. The barrier remained elsewhere, solid and cold. Only here, a patch no wider than a man's shoulders, offered passage. Not freedom, but a path into the Witch's domain. Hope, poisoned with terror, grew in the village hall. A desperate plan formed. They had to try. They had to reach her. They had to end it. Ten were chosen: Finn for his knowledge of old tales, Marta the blacksmith for her strength, Thomas the carpenter for his steady hand, and seven others, their faces grim with fear and resolve. Axes, hammers, hunting knives, and Finn's rusted sword – these were their weapons against centuries of malice. The rest would stay, guard the village, pray. If the hunters failed, or if the Witch struck Briar's End while they were gone…no one spoke of that.

The forest swallowed them whole. The air thickened, it was damp and there was a putrid smell, sharp and metallic. The trees here weren't just old; they felt sentient. Knots watched like eyes. Roots snaked across the narrow, overgrown path, tripping them. Every rustle in the undergrowth sounded deliberate. Every snapped twig echoed like a gunshot. The light filtering through the dense canopy was weak, green-tinged, casting long, distorted shadows that seemed to twist and turn. Thomas swore he saw pale figures moving swiftly between the trunks, vanishing when he looked directly. Marta gripped her heavy hammer until her knuckles cracked. The oppressive silence pressed down, broken only by their ragged breathing and the crunch of their own footsteps. Fear was a living thing, coiling around them, an entity following them wherever they went. They moved in tight formation, weapons ready, eyes darting. The path seemed endless, winding deeper into a suffocating heart of darkness. The unnatural stillness amplified every sound, every heartbeat.

Hours bled together in the gloom. They were exhausted and afraid. Then, a shift. The trees thinned abruptly. They stood at the edge of a small, unnatural clearing. No birds sang here, no insects buzzed. In the center stood the cabin. It wasn't derelict; it wasn't right. Something about the cabin seemed *wrong*. It was built from wood blackened like charred bone, its angles seemed slightly off, making the eyes ache. The single window, dark and dust-caked, felt like a blind eye. A heavy, warped door hung slightly ajar. No smoke rose from the crooked chimney. A low, constant hum vibrated through the air, a physical pressure against their skin. It came from the cabin. The smell intensified – decay, metal, and beneath it, a sweetness like rotting honey. This was the place. The source of their torment. Finn raised a shaking hand, signaling the others to fan out. Weapons were lifted. Their hearts beating hard in their chests.

Marta stepped forward first, her hammer held high. "Witch!" Her voice, loud in the silence, cracked slightly. "Show yourself! Your quarrel is with ghosts! Let Briar's End go!" There was only silence, it lingered in the thickness of the air. The hum deepened. Thomas edged towards the open door, axe ready. He peered into the gloom. There was only darkness, thick, tangible. The hum resonated louder from within. He took a step onto the sagging porch. The wood creaked like a wounded beast under his feet. He pushed the door wider. It scraped open with a sound like tearing flesh.

The interior was a single room, bare and filthy. Dust coated everything. In the center of the packed earth floor, a single candle burned with a sickly yellow flame that didn't flicker despite the open door. No one was there. But the hum was deafening now, vibrating through their boots. The sweet-rot smell choked them. Finn pointed a trembling finger towards the far corner. A thick, knotted rug lay bunched, revealing the edge of a heavy trapdoor beneath it. The hum pulsed strongest from there. Thomas and another villager, Jory, moved towards it, axes raised. They dragged the rug aside. The trapdoor was solid, bound with cold iron. Jory grabbed the iron ring and heaved. It opened with a shriek of rusted hinges, revealing stone steps descending into utter blackness. A wave of frigid, foul air washed over them.

"Don't!" Finn groaned, but it was too late. A figure materialized from the shadows beside the open trapdoor. One moment, empty space; the next, *her*. She was short, thin, draped in ragged, earth-colored cloth. Her skin wasn't wrinkled, but stretched tight over her shape, the color of damp parchment. Her hair hung in lank, gray braids. But her eyes…they glowed with the same sickly yellow as the candle flame, holding depths of pure, ancient malice. A chill radiated from her, colder than the deepest winter. The humming seemed to emanate from her very being.

"You trespass." Her voice was dry, echoing inside their skulls, bypassing their ears. It held no anger, only cold, infinite contempt. "The debt remains unpaid. Your blood still carries the stain."

"Your enemies are dust!" Thomas shouted, brandishing his axe, trying to hide his terror with fury. "We have done nothing to you!"

"Nothing?" The Witch tilted her head. A dry, clicking sound came from her neck. "Your walls stand on stolen ground. Your breath draws air fouled by their lies. The blood debt flows through your veins, generation to generation. It never ends. It feeds the roots." She raised a hand, skeletal fingers ending in points like thorns. The candle flame flared, casting long, leaping shadows that seemed to grasp at the villagers near the door. Marta screamed as an unseen force wrenched the hammer from her grip. It clattered harmlessly against the far wall. Finn lunged forward with his sword. The blade passed through the Witch as if she weren't there, meeting only icy air. He stumbled, falling to his knees.

Panic exploded. Jory swung his axe wildly at the figure. It connected with nothing, throwing him off balance. Another villager, Mara, threw a heavy stone from the doorway. It flew straight through the Witch's chest and shattered against the back wall. The Witch didn't flinch. Her yellow eyes fixed on Jory as he scrambled to his feet. She pointed a single, thorn-like finger. Jory froze, a strangled gasp escaped him. His skin began to gray, tightening over his bones. His eyes widened, then dulled, turning the same sickly yellow as the Witch's. He crumbled inward, collapsing into a pile of dry, gray dust that scattered across the dirt floor. A collective scream ripped from the remaining villagers. Horror, pure and absolute, washed over them. Their weapons were useless.

"Run!" Finn screamed, scrambling backwards. "Back to the village!" They turned, a desperate, terrified stampede for the door. The Witch moved. She didn't walk; she flowed, a blur of ragged cloth and bone-pale skin. She was before them, blocking the doorway. Her presence was a physical weight, pressing them back. The humming intensified, vibrating their teeth and bones. The air crackled with unseen energy. The open trapdoor behind them seemed to exhale a deeper cold, a deeper darkness.

"You sought my heart," the Witch hissed, her voice slithering into their minds. "You found it. Below." Her burning gaze swept over them. "The curse needs feeding. The roots hunger." She gestured towards the open darkness of the trapdoor. "Your fear is sweet. Your despair sustains. But your flesh...your flesh will nourish the deep earth. Become part of the forest. Forever."

An invisible force seized them. It wasn't hands; it was the air itself turning solid, cold, and relentless. It dragged them backwards, towards the open pit, feet scrabbling uselessly on the dirt floor. They screamed, fought, clawed at the air. Marta grabbed the doorframe, her muscles straining. The wood splintered under her fingers. Thomas swung his axe wildly at nothing, tears of terror streaming down his face. Finn stared into the Witch's glowing eyes, seeing centuries of hatred, an ocean of pain that would never end. "Please!" he choked. "Mercy!"

"Mercy died with my children," the Witch said, her voice devoid of inflection. "In the fire your ancestors lit. Burned for herbs they called 'witchcraft'. Burned for daring to heal." The force intensified. Marta was ripped from the doorway. They were pulled towards the darkness. One by one, they tumbled over the edge, into the blackness of the trapdoor. Their screams echoed up the stone steps, abruptly cut short. Then, silence. Only the constant, low hum remained.

The Witch stood motionless in the center of the room. The candle flame burned steady. She turned her burning gaze towards the open door, looking through the trees, towards Briar's End. A faint, cruel smile spread across her face. It was gone in an instant. She gestured. The trapdoor slammed shut with a final, echoing thud. The heavy rug slithered back over it. The cabin door creaked slowly closed, blotting out the weak forest light. The hum softened, settling back into the bones of the earth. The forest waited. The roots were fed. For now.

Back in Briar's End, the villagers guarding the perimeter felt the air grow colder. They saw nothing. They heard nothing from the forest. But the barrier remained, colder, harder than ever. The unnatural twilight deepened. They looked towards the forest edge, towards the crack Old Man Finn had found, and knew. The hunters were gone. The Witch remained. And the Thorned Path had only led deeper into the dark. The hunger of the roots was patient. It would wait for the next desperate soul.

Whisperroot

The forest behind Dallow's Hill didn't exist on any map.

Locals called it Dead Holler. They warned about the silence. No birds. No wind. Just trees that grew too close together, their branches twisted like fingers. It was the kind of place you didn't look at too long. People said the forest took things. Animals. Time. People.

Seventeen children had vanished there over the last forty years. Mary Cartwright was nine when her sister, Annie, disappeared. They'd gone into the woods after school. Just a dare. Mary stayed on the path, Annie didn't. She followed a voice. It was soft. It said her name. It came from the dark between the trees. She laughed and stepped off the trail. Then she was gone. No snap of branches, no scream, no sound, just gone.

Mary ran home alone. She told the police. They searched for weeks. They found nothing.

That was sixteen years ago.

Mary returned to Dallow's Hill when her father died. The house was still the same. The woods still pressed against the backyard like a bruise that never faded. She couldn't sleep the first night back. Something scratched at the windows. She checked, nothing was there. Just shadows between the trees.

The next morning, she found a small footprint in the mud beneath her window, barefoot, small. A child's. Her hands shook as she measured it. The size matched Annie's when she vanished.

She didn't tell anyone. She didn't leave. She began hearing the voice again. "Mary…"

It came from the trees. It came every night.

She bought a flashlight and a flare gun. She left the back porch and stepped into Dead Holler.

The forest swallowed sound. Her boots made no noise. The air felt thick. Her flashlight beam died after ten feet. The trees leaned in. She walked for an hour, turning back often. But the house was already gone.

The ground dipped. She found herself on a path, narrow and soft, lined with leaves that didn't crunch under her feet. She followed it until she reached a clearing. At the center stood a girl in a white dress. Her hair hung in tangles. Her arms dangled at her sides.

She looked up.

It was Annie.

The same age as when she vanished. Face pale, eyes hollow, no blinking, no smile.

"Annie?" Mary's voice cracked.

The girl didn't speak. She turned and walked into the trees. Mary followed.

They moved deeper. The air grew colder. Hands reached from the ground, thin, gray, fingers twitching. They didn't grab—yet. They waited.

The girl stopped at a ring of stones. Each stone had a name scratched into it. Mary saw one with her father's name. One with her mother's. One with her own.

The girl pointed at it.

Mary stepped back. She raised the flare gun. "You're not Annie."

The girl smiled. Her lips split wide. Her eyes turned black. The trees groaned, skeletal branches reaching for anything or nothing. Just reaching.

Dozens of children stepped from the trunks, all pale, all hollow, none breathing.

The hands in the dirt started to move.

Mary ran.

The trees moved too. They shifted, closed, changed the path. She fired the flare into the sky. It hit a branch, set nothing ablaze. The light died before it reached the clouds. The forest swallowed it.

She tripped over a root and hit the ground. Hands grabbed her ankle, cold, wet. She kicked free and crawled to her feet. The children didn't follow, they watched.

She found the edge. The tree line opened for one moment. Her house stood ahead. Her porch light flickered.

She burst through the trees.

Then stopped.

The house was empty, no windows, no doors, just a shell. A girl stood in the yard, white dress, tangle of hair, different face. Mary turned back. The forest was gone. Replaced by a blackness darker than night.

No sound. No wind. Just cold.

Then came the whispers. They poured from the ground. From the sky. From her own mouth. She screamed. But it made no sound. When she woke, she stood in the clearing again. The girl was gone. The stones remained. Her name was still on one.

So was another: *Claire Atwell.*

Claire was ten. Lived two houses down. Loved puzzles. She vanished the next day. Her parents found her shoes in the hallway, muddy. Her window open.

Mary tried to warn people. No one believed her. The police recommended her to doctors, specialists. They ran tests, gave her pills. Locked her in for observation.

The night she was discharged, she walked back into Dead Holler.

She never came out.

Weeks passed.

The town sealed the trail.

But the whispers didn't stop.

Children still heard them.

Sometimes late at night, parents would wake to see their kids standing at the window, eyes blank, smiling.

One girl disappeared during breakfast. In front of her family. One blink, and she was gone. Only her spoon remained.

The forest was alive now, bigger, closer.

One afternoon, two hikers found a clearing deep in the woods. At the center stood a circle of children, all dressed in white, all staring. One girl stood in the middle, hair tangled, eyes empty, skin pale.

She looked nine.

She wore Mary's face.

Béla Lugosi Meets Count Dracula

I

Stone pressed cold against the ancient castle. High in the Carpathians, the air was stale and thin. A Mist clung to the towers like a shroud, thrown over it by the wind. Inside, only darkness. Dust lay thick on broken furniture. Tapestries hung torn, almost shredded from age, their colors long faded. Only the central hall showed signs of use. A fire smoldered low in the massive fire place, casting shifting shadows on the walls. It gave no warmth.

Count Dracula stood by a high window. He stared into the swirling gray outside. His face held no expression. He saw the mountains, the deep forests, the villages far below. He saw centuries. Time meant little here. Only hunger and the deep quiet of darkness. His stillness was absolute. He stood as if he were a statue carved from night itself.

Footsteps broke the silence. They were hesitant, scraping on the stone floor. Igor entered the hall. He moved like a shadow too afraid of the light. His frame was thin, shoulders hunched. His eyes darted around the room, avoiding the figure by the window. He clutched a large envelope. His hands trembled.

"My Lord," Igor whispered. His voice cracked.

Dracula did not turn. The silence filled the room. Igor swallowed hard.

"My Lord," he tried again, louder. "A thing...a thing has come."

Slowly, Dracula turned. His movement was fluid, silent. His eyes fixed on Igor. They were dark, depthless. Igor flinched.

"What thing?" Dracula's voice was low. It filled the space, cold and heavy.

Igor shuffled forward. He held out the envelope. "From the world below, Master. From...America." He spat the last word like poison. "Men brought it. Traders. Passing through the valley. They spoke of...pictures. Moving pictures."

Dracula's gaze shifted to the envelope. He did not take it. "Pictures."

"Of...of you, Master." Igor trembled harder. "Or...something pretending."

A flicker passed through Dracula's eyes, not anger, not yet. Curiosity. Cold, sharp curiosity. He extended a hand. Long fingers, pale. Igor placed the envelope into it, then stepped back quickly.

Dracula tore the flap. He pulled out several large, glossy sheets. Photographs. He held one up to the dim firelight.

The image showed a man. A man with a sharp widow's peak, dark hair swept back. Heavy-lidded eyes stared intensely from the paper. The man wore a high-collared cloak. He stood rigid, aristocratic. Behind him, a painted backdrop suggested a castle corridor.

Dracula stared. His face remained impassive. He examined the sharp lines of the face, the dramatic pose. He turned to the next image. The same man, closer now, eyes piercing the viewer, a faint, unnatural smile on thin lips. Another image showed the man reaching out with a slow, deliberate hand gesture.

"Who?" Dracula groaned.

Igor flinched again. "They...they call him Béla Lugosi, Master. An actor. From Hungary, they said. But now...in America. He...he plays..." Igor trailed off, unable to say it.

"He plays me." Dracula stated it, flat, final. He looked again at the image. At the cape, the stare, the posture. An imitation. A cheap copy. Mortal flesh pretending to be night eternal. The first spark ignited. Deep within, cold embers began to glow.

He shuffled through the other photographs. Each one showed this "Lugosi" in the role. Posing. Performing. Staring out with borrowed menace. Dracula's lips pressed into a thin line. The cold embers flared, hotter now. This wasn't mere curiosity, this was...recognition twisted. His own image, stolen. Paraded before the world by a fraud. Reduced to entertainment.

The stillness in the hall changed. It wasn't quiet anymore. It was pressure, building. The air felt thick, charged. Dust motes seemed to freeze in the gloom. Igor pressed himself against a stone pillar, trying to vanish.

Dracula's hand tightened on the photographs. The glossy paper crumpled. "Where?" His voice was a low vibration, colder than the mountain wind.

"My Lord?" Igor whispered.

"Where do they show this...this...mockery?"

"The town, Master. Braşov. They...they have a building. A *cinema*. They show the moving pictures there. Every night, the traders said."

"Tonight?"

Igor nodded frantically. "Yes, Master. Tonight. They said...it is popular."

Dracula let the crumpled photographs fall to the stone floor. They landed without a sound. He turned his gaze fully on Igor. The depthless eyes held a new light. A cold, focused light. "Take me."

"Master?" Igor stammered.

"To this cinema. Tonight. I will see this performance. I must see this for myself."

Igor's face drained of what little color it had left. "But...the town... people...it is dangerous, Master!"

A ghost of a smile ran across Dracula's lips. Then it faded into the darkness. "For them. Prepare the coach. We leave at moonrise."

The journey was swift. The black coach, drawn by horses as dark as the night itself, flew down the mountain road. Mist parted before it. Dracula sat inside, a shadow within shadows. Igor drove, hunched and shivering despite the thick coat he wore. The lights of Braşov appeared below, small yellow points against the vast darkness.

They entered the town. It felt cramped, noisy, and smelled of coal smoke and humanity. Dracula recoiled inwardly. The cinema was easy to find. A garish sign flashed "*DRACULA*" in large letters. People crowded the entrance. Laughter and excited chatter filled the air. The sight of mortals eagerly lining up to see a travesty of his existence stoked the cold fire inside him.

They did not join the crowd. Dracula moved like smoke. He flowed through a side alley, unseen. Igor followed, whimpering softly. They found a rusted metal door at the rear of the building. Dracula placed a hand on the lock. The metal groaned, then snapped under his strength. The door swung open silently.

Inside, it was dark and smelled of dust and hot machinery. They were in the projection booth. A small, round man jumped, dropping a reel of film. He opened his mouth to shout. Dracula's hand shot out, clamping over his mouth. His eyes met the man's. The projectionist's scream died in his throat. His eyes glazed over. He slumped to the floor, unconscious. Igor dragged the body into a corner.

Below, through a small window, the cinema auditorium spread out. Rows of seats faced a large white screen. The room buzzed with anticipation. Dracula ignored the audience. His focus was absolute. His focus was the screen.

The projector clattered to life. Light cut through the dusty air, hitting the screen. Music swelled from speakers below. Titles appeared: "*DRACULA*." Then, the image of a stagecoach rattling through mountains. Dracula watched. His face was stone.

Then, the coach arrived at a castle gate. The door creaked open. A figure stood there, holding a lamp. He was tall, cloaked. The face turned slowly towards the audience. The widow's peak. Intense eyes. It was Dracula's nemesis Béla Lugosi.

A murmur of awe and fear rippled through the audience. Dracula felt nothing but cold contempt.

He watched the imitation move. Slow, deliberate, unnatural pauses. Dracula leaned closer to the booth window. His knuckles were white where he gripped the ledge too tight.

"I don't do that," he whispered, his voice barely audible over the film's sound. On screen, Lugosi extended a hand with theatrical slowness.

Lugosi spoke. His voice, amplified, filled the hall. Heavy accent. Measured, unnatural cadence. "I am...Dracula." The audience gasped.

"I don't say that," Dracula hissed. The words were cold as ice. "I do not announce myself like a cheap carnival act."

He watched the imitation interact with mortals. The piercing stare. The unnatural stillness. The affected gestures. Each moment was a fresh insult, a reduction, a lie performed for sheep. The cold fire within Dracula's being burned hotter, brighter. It was rage now. Pure, focused rage.

Then came the weaknesses. Renfield babbling about protection. Van Helsing brandishing a crucifix. The imitation recoiling, hissing, showing fear.

Dracula let out a breath, a heavy sigh. His eyes narrowed to slits. On screen, Lugosi shrank from the symbol, face contorted.

A low growl rumbled in Dracula's chest. Igor flinched beside him, pressing himself flat against the wall.

Sunlight. The imitation avoided it. Feared it. The film showed it as a deadly force.

The stake. Van Helsing spoke of it as the ultimate weapon.

Dracula watched, motionless. But the air in the booth crackled. The unconscious projectionist stirred, moaned, then fell still again. The metal casing of the projector felt suddenly colder.

The film ended. Applause erupted below. People chattered excitedly as the lights came up. They filed out, buzzing about the horror, the performance, the Count.

Dracula remained frozen at the window. The screen was blank now, white and empty. Like the void in his chest filled only with fury. The applause faded. The cinema emptied. Silence returned.

Igor dared to move. He crept forward. "Master?" His voice was dry and harsh.

Dracula turned. His face was terrible. Not twisted in anger, but set in lines of absolute, unfriendly fury. His eyes burned with dark fire. Igor stumbled back.

"That...that creature," Dracula said. The words were precise, each one as a shard of ice. "That performer. Lugosi. He has made me a joke. A thing of rules. A thing to be *feared* by trinkets and daylight." He paused. The silence screamed. "He has told the world how to kill me."

Igor trembled violently. "It...it is just a story, Master! A foolish play!"

"Stories have power, Igor," Dracula stated. His voice was deadly quiet. "Belief has power. He has sown seeds. Seeds of defiance. He has shown them the shape of their fear, and in doing so, given them a target. He has made me...manageable." He spat the words. "This cannot stand."

Igor wrung his hands. "Perhaps...perhaps the courts, Master? A lawsuit? Defamation? We could—"

Dracula's hand shot out, not touching Igor, but the servant froze as if gripped by an invisible fist. "Courts?" Dracula's laugh was short, harsh, like a stone breaking. "Mortal laws? For this? This is blood-deep. This demands blood payment." He released the unseen hold. Igor sagged, gasping.

Dracula looked away, back towards the blank screen. His mind raced, cold and calculating. The imitation's face, the voice, the weakness displayed – they burned in his mind. This actor, this mortal, sat safe in a land of sun, profiting from his image, eroding his true power. Spreading lies that could become weapons.

The solution formed, clear, absolute, personal.

"He lives," Dracula said. "In that place of false light. That factory of dreams."

"Hollywood, Master," Igor supplied weakly.

Dracula nodded once. "Yes. Hollywood." He turned fully now, his cloak swirling in the dusty air of the booth. His eyes fixed on a point far beyond the walls, beyond the mountains, across the vast ocean. "Prepare for a long journey, Igor. We go to America. We go to Hollywood."

He stepped towards the broken door, the darkness clinging to him like a second skin. The final words fell, heavy and final as a tombstone sealing shut.

"I will have a conversation with Mr. Lugosi."

The cold certainty in his voice was more terrifying than any shout. Igor stared after the vanishing shape of his master, knowing the conversation would only end one way. The night outside seemed to deepen, swallowing the town whole. The journey had begun.

II

The castle felt too small now. Stone walls that had contained centuries now seemed to close in. Dracula paced the central hall, each step echoed. The crumpled photographs still lay on the floor where he'd dropped them. Lugosi's stolen face stared up from the stone, mocking.

Igor watched from the shadows near the fire place. He flinched with every turn his master made. The air popped and crackled, not with heat, but with cold purpose. Dracula stopped. He faced Igor.

"Passage," Dracula said. "To America. To California. Discreet."

Igor swallowed. "The sea, Master? Sunlight...the water..."

"Not on deck." Dracula's voice cut him off. "Below. Hidden. A box. Sealed. Tight." He gestured sharply. "Large enough for me. And earth. Earth from my crypt. Enough to fill the bottom."

Igor understood. The thought chilled his blood. "A...coffin ship, Master?"

139

"Call it what you like. Find a vessel. Cargo. Unremarkable. Pay whatever the rats demand. But it must leave soon. Within days."

Igor scurried out into the misty courtyard. Dracula turned back to the window. Beyond the mountains, beyond the sea, lay Hollywood. And Lugosi. The imitation's face burned in his mind. The slow hand. The hissed words. The recoil from the cross. Each memory was a fresh cut. The rage settled deep, cold and hard as the Carpathian rock. He needed to move. Now.

The ship was old. The iron hull creaked incessantly. It smelled of salt, rust, and old water. *The Star of Gdańsk*. A Polish freighter bound for New York, then onward through the Panama Canal to Los Angeles. Igor had paid triple. The captain asked no questions. Gold silenced his curiosity.

The crate waited in the deepest hold. Thick, rough-hewn oak planks. Iron bands reinforced the corners. It stood taller than a man, wider than a door. Workers had grumbled while loading it. It was heavy, unusually heavy. They nailed the lid shut under Igor's watchful eye. Inside, a thick layer of dark, damp earth covered the bottom. The smell of ancient stone and grave mold filled the enclosed space.

Dracula stood within the earth. He wore simple, dark clothes, no cloak. He looked up at the nailed-down lid. Only inches above his head. The darkness was absolute. It was thick, suffocating. He heard the workers' muffled curses, the thud of hammers driving nails. Then, silence. Distant clangs. The creaks and groans of the ship. The thrum of engines starting.

The crate shifted. A deep vibration ran through the wood. They were moving.

Dracula lowered himself. He sat in the earth. He pulled his knees close. The space allowed little else. He could not stand. He could not stretch. He could barely shift his weight. The wood pressed in on all sides. It was complete darkness. Silence, except for the ship's incessant creaking and the slosh of water against the hull far below.

He closed his eyes. It made no difference. The dark was inside and out. Time ceased. There was only the box. The pressure. The smell of wood, iron, and his own crypt.

Hunger stirred, a dull ache, deep within. He ignored it. He had learned to control his hunger long ago. He focused on the dark.

Lugosi's face surfaced. The piercing stare from the photograph. The arrogant tilt of the head. *I am...Dracula.* The slow, deliberate extension of the hand. Dracula's own hand clenched in the confined space. Nails dug into his palm. *I don't do that.* The fury was like a cold knot in his gut.

The image shifted. Lugosi flinching, hissing, backing away from Van Helsing's cross. Fear in those borrowed eyes. Weakness. *I would never say that. I would never show that.* The knot in his gut grew heavier, colder. He had ruled the night for centuries. Feared by whispers, not by props. Now? A cheap trick. A blueprint for defiance. *He has told them how to kill me.* The thought fed his fury.

Hours bled into days. The ship creaked, rolled. Water crashed against the hull. Dracula remained motionless. The hunger sharpened. It became a constant gnawing, a hollow fire in his veins. Thirst joined it. A dry scraping in his throat. He needed blood. Life. He had nothing. Only the dark, the wood, the earth.

He tried to sleep. True sleep, the death-sleep. It wouldn't come. The confinement was too absolute. The rage too bright. The ship's movements were unpredictable jolts, preventing true rest. He existed in a limbo. Awake in the dark, trapped.

He replayed the film. Frame by agonizing frame. Lugosi's every gesture, every line. The slow walk. The unnatural pauses. The theatrical menace. Dracula dissected it. Each element was an insult. A reduction of his power to a stage act. The audience's gasps, their fearful delight – it echoed in his prison. Mortals entertained by his defilement.

The crate felt smaller. The air tasted stale, thick with dust and the scent of the earth. His own breath sounded loud. His heartbeat, a slow, heavy drum in the silence. The hunger screamed. It was a physical pain now, twisting his insides. He felt weaker. The relentless pressure of the wood above, the walls around him, pressed on his mind. It was a torment worse than any physical wound. Centuries of freedom, now caged like an animal. For this. For an actor's vanity.

Days turned into weeks. The engine drone changed pitch. The ship's movements grew calmer. Warmer air seeped through the wood. Different smells. Oil. Machinery. A strange, dry scent. Land. America. He knew they neared the canal. Then, the open Pacific. More days of rocking darkness.

The hunger was a constant agony. A gnawing void that consumed his thoughts. His skin felt paper-thin. His vision, though useless in the dark, felt sharper, hungrier. He imagined blood. Rivers of it. The hot, coppery taste. The life flooding into him. He imagined Lugosi's blood. Pictured the actor's throat. The pulse point. The terror in his eyes as the life drained away. *That* was the only script that mattered now.

The crate became his world, his universe, wood, earth, dark, hunger, rage and the flickering, hated image of Béla Lugosi. They were all he had. They fused together. The confinement fed the fury. The fury burned against the confinement. It forged him. Tempered his purpose into something sharp and deadly.

Finally, a different kind of movement. Slower. Shouts filtered down, faint but clear. Different languages. Dock sounds. Clanging. Whistles. The ship shuddered to a stop. Heavy footsteps overhead. Dracula listened. He heard the crate being hooked. Felt the lurch as it lifted, it swung. The world tilted slowly as he was moved in the crate. He braced himself against the earth. The crate landed with a heavy thud on solid ground. Then, rolling. Wheels on pavement. He was moved. Lifted again. The rumble of an engine. A truck. They were driving.

Sunlight. He felt it. A deadly pressure, even through the thick wood. A faint warmth, a searing potential just beyond the planks. It beat against his prison like a physical force. Day. He was helpless. Trapped in the crate, sensing the killing light inches away. He pressed deeper into the earth. His prison was now his only shield.

The truck drove for a long time. The sounds changed. City noises faded. The air inside the crate grew warmer, drier. Dustier. The truck stopped. More movement. The crate lifted. It was carried. Set down, indoors. The deadly pressure of the sun vanished, replaced by the stale quiet of an enclosed space. A door closed, locks clicked. Footsteps retreated.

It was complete silence. Thick, dusty silence.

Dracula remained still. He listened. There was nothing. Only his own shallow breath. The frantic beat of his starved heart. The house was empty. It was all pre-arranged. Secluded. He knew without seeing. He was in Los Angeles. In Hollywood. But the sun still reigned. He was still caged.

He waited, motionless. The hunger was a living thing now, tearing at his insides. His thirst was a desert in his throat. Weeks of deprivation had hollowed him. He felt thin, brittle. But the rage burned brighter, hotter, fueled by the agony. It was the only thing holding him together. The image of Lugosi's face, smug on the screen, kept the fire alive.

He measured time by the fading heat outside the crate. By the deepening shadows he sensed even through the wood. The sun was setting. The lethal day was ending.

Darkness gathered. True night approached. Dracula felt it like a cooling balm. A promise of release, the pressure lessened. The world outside his wooden tomb shifted.

He stretched his senses, reached out. The house was empty, the grounds outside were still. Night had fallen, deep, complete night.

He moved. For the first time in weeks, he shifted his weight. Stiff muscles protested, joints cracked. He placed his hands flat against the heavy lid above him, oak, thick, nailed shut with iron bands.

He gathered the cold fury, the burning hunger. The weeks of torment in the dark. He focused it all into his arms, his shoulders. Every ounce of strength left in his starved body. It wasn't just physical, it was centuries of power, concentrated. It was vengeance, demanding release.

He pushed.

The wood creaked and groaned. A deep, protesting sound. Nails shrieked as they bent, iron bands strained. Dracula pushed harder. A snarl escaped his lips, raw and guttural.

With a splintering crash, the lid exploded outward. Shattered oak planks flew across the dusty floor of the small, bare room. Iron bands snapped like dry twigs. Earth spilled over the edges of the crate.

Dracula stood. He unfolded himself from the broken box. He stood tall in the unfamiliar darkness. His movements were stiff, jerky. He stepped out onto the wooden floorboards, leaving footprints of dark soil.

Moonlight filtered through a grimy window. It fell upon him. He was gaunt. His face was a death mask of skin stretched tight over his sharp cheekbones, pulled thin across his skull. His eyes burned, not with their usual dark depth, but with a fierce, unnatural light. Hunger and fury radiated from him. His clothes hung loose on his frame. He looked like famine given form, like vengeance clawed from the grave.

He breathed the air. It was dry and warm. It was filled with alien scents – dust, gasoline, strange plants, the distant tang of the ocean. A world away from the damp stone and pine of the Carpathians. This was indeed Hollywood.

He tilted his head, listening. The night sounds were all wrong. Crickets and distant traffic. A dog barking. There were no wolves, no wind in ancient pines. It was a foreign night. A false night.

But it was night. His domain.

He took a step. Then another. His legs trembled. Weakness from the voyage, from starvation, threatened to buckle him. He locked his knees. He focused on the fire in his eyes. On the face burned into his mind.

Lugosi.

The name became a silent snarl on his cracked lips. The actor was here. Somewhere in this sprawling city of false light. He was close. Dracula could almost taste the fear he would inspire. Almost feel the hot blood.

He needed strength. He needed blood. He needed it soon. The hunger screamed inside him, a physical pain sharper than any blade. He couldn't face Lugosi like this. Not yet. First, sustenance. Then, the reckoning.

He moved towards the window. He looked out. He saw unfamiliar shapes of palm trees against the night sky, the glow of electric lights in the distance. The city pulsed, it was alive, full of prey.

A thin, predatory smile came across Dracula's dried lips. There was no warmth in his smile, only hunger, only promise.

He turned from the window. His burning eyes scanned the dark room, the shattered crate, the spilled earth of his homeland. He was here. In the land of the imitation. The hunt could begin.

First, he needed to feed.

144

III

The hunger drove him first. Dracula moved through the unfamiliar Los Angeles night. He was a gaunt shadow. The city lights were harsh, yellow, white, electric. They hurt his eyes. The air tasted of exhaust and dust. He smelled food everywhere, warm bodies, blood. The scent was maddening.

He found prey near the river, a man sleeping rough under a bridge. Dracula was upon him before the man woke. The feeding was swift, silent, desperate. The blood was thin, poor quality, but it was life. It flowed into his starved veins. His strength returned. Not full strength, not yet but enough.

He fed again. A woman walking alone. Her fear was sharp, sweet. Her blood was richer. Each victim restored him. Filled the hollows the voyage carved. His skin lost some of its papery thinness. His movements regained fluidity. The gauntness remained. The burning in his eyes intensified, he was focused.

He learned, he listened, he watched. Hollywood was a machine. It was loud, bright, obsessed with itself. Newspapers fluttered in gutters. Headlines screamed about *"DRACULA"* and *"LUGOSI."* He saw Lugosi's stolen face everywhere. It was on posters, in shop windows, grinning from newsprint.

The imitation was busy, promoting the lie. Dracula discovered Lugosi's schedule. A premiere here. A personal appearance there. A radio interview. The mortal played his role. Enjoyed the stolen fame.

Dracula prepared. He needed to blend. Mortal eyes must not see the predator too soon. He found a tailor. It was late at night, the tailor was alone. Dracula entered. The man looked up. He saw the intense eyes, the unnatural paleness of his face. He opened his mouth to protest the late hour.

He never closed it.

Dracula left wearing fine evening clothes. A black tailcoat, white shirt, high collar, crisp trousers. He looked like wealth, like aristocracy. He looked like the image Lugosi had stolen from him, but sharper, real. The clothes fit his lean frame perfectly. He discarded the bloodstained rags he'd arrived in.

He attended the next event. It was at a grand theater, Lugosi was appearing after a screening. Dracula arrived late, he stood at the very back. The crowd buzzed, excited, fearful but in a safe, thrilling way. When the film ended, applause shook the building. The lights came up.

Lugosi walked on stage, applause swelled, he bowed, dramatic. He wore his Dracula costume, cape, makeup, widow's peak painted on. He raised his hands. Silence fell. He spoke. That slow, accented cadence. *"I bid you welcome..."*

Dracula watched. Cold fury settled deep within him. He saw the pretension in Lugosi's movements. The theatrical menace, the cheap imitation of power. Mortals gasped, clapped. They were enthralled by the counterfeit.

Lugosi worked the crowd. He answered questions, signed autographs, he posed. He gave them the performance they craved. The imitation Dracula.

Dracula moved. He didn't push, he flowed. People parted without knowing why. He moved down the aisle. He was silent, unnoticed until he was close. He stopped near the front. He stood perfectly still. He was like a statue of darkness in formal wear, his eyes were fixed on Lugosi.

Lugosi saw him. Mid-signature, he glanced up. His practiced smile faltered. He saw the man, the intense gaze, the unnatural stillness. The sharp, pale face. The clothes that mirrored his own costume, but somehow looked more real, more dangerous. Lugosi blinked. For a second, the actor dropped the act, confusion flickered across his face. Then the mask snapped back. He looked away, dismissed it as an exceptionally dedicated fan, an impersonator. Hollywood was full of them.

But he felt the gaze. It followed him. It was heavy, unblinking. Even when he looked away, he felt it. A cold spot on his skin. He finished the appearance quickly. He left the stage. The applause followed him.

Dracula watched him go. He turned. Melted back into the departing crowd, unseen.

He stalked him, night after night. Lugosi attended a party at a producer's mansion. Dracula stood on the terrace, watching through French doors. Lugosi laughed, drank champagne, held court. He felt the chill, saw the pale figure outside. He looked away, told himself it was nothing, nerves.

Lugosi did a radio interview. Dracula stood across the street. Hidden in the doorway of a closed shop. He watched Lugosi enter the building. He heard his amplified voice later, drifting from an open window. *"...the children of the night..."* Dracula's lip curled. This was more mockery.

The gaze was constant, relentless. Lugosi started seeing it everywhere. In his car mirror, reflected in a shop window, a pale face in the crowd. He was always watching, always silent, always intense. It unnerved him. The character he played began to feel less like a role and more like a target.

He hired extra security, men who looked tough. They scanned crowds. They saw nothing unusual. Dracula moved like smoke. He watched the guards. Lugosi's contemptuous, mortal shields.

Lugosi went to his dressing room after a theater show, he felt drained. The constant feeling of being watched grated him. He dismissed his driver. He wanted a moment alone. He walked out the stage door into the narrow alley behind the theater. There were trash cans, dumpsters. The smell of grease paint and garbage assaulted his senses.

He lit a cigarette. Took a deep drag. The night air felt cool. He leaned against the brick wall, closed his eyes. He tried to shake off the unease.

"You perform well."

The voice came from the darkness. It was quiet, cold, precise. It was a hungarian accent, but deeper, real. It was not the stage cadence Lugosi had become accustomed to.

Lugosi jumped. He dropped his cigarette, spun around.

Dracula stood ten feet away. He hadn't been there a second before. He emerged from the deeper shadows near a dumpster. His formal clothes were immaculate. His face was bone-white in the weak alley light. His eyes burned.

Lugosi's heart hammered. Annoyance mixed with sudden fear. "Who are you? What do you want? Autograph? Photo? It is late. Go away." He tried for his stage voice, commanding, it wavered.

Dracula took a step forward, silent. "I want," he said, each word distinct, "what is mine."

Lugosi frowned. He was confused, aggravated. "Yours? What are you talking about? Get lost before I call the police." He reached for the stage door handle.

"You stole my face," Dracula stated. "My identity. My name. You paraded it. Reduced it. Made it a...joke." The last word was a hiss.

Lugosi paused. He stared. Recognition dawned, warped by disbelief. The intense eyes, the paleness, the accent, the clothes. The man from the crowds. "You...you are mad," Lugosi said, a nervous laugh escaped him. "You think you are Dracula? The character? From Stoker? It is fiction! A story! Vampires? They are not real!" He gestured dismissively. "Go home. Sleep it off."

Dracula moved. One second he was ten feet away. The next, he was directly in front of Lugosi. No blur, just...there. His hand shot out. It closed on Lugosi's throat, not crushing, just holding, immobilizing.

Lugosi gasped. He tried to pull away. Dracula's grip was like iron. It was cold, unyielding. He stared into the burning eyes inches from his own. The reality hit him, hard. The speed, the strength, the impossible coldness of the hand. His eyes widened. Pure terror flooded him. "N-no..."

"Fiction?" Dracula whispered. His breath smelled of dust and old blood. "You showed them weakness. Fear of crosses." He nodded towards the theater door. A small crucifix was painted on the stage door for luck. Lugosi instinctively looked at it. Dracula followed his gaze. He looked back at Lugosi. A cold smile ran across his face. "Watch."

He released Lugosi's throat. Stepped towards the painted cross on the door. He reached out, deliberately. He pressed his bare palm flat against the crude symbol.

There was a sizzle. Smoke curled from his hand. The smell of burning flesh filled the alley.

Lugosi gagged. He stumbled back. Horror choked him.

Dracula held his hand there. His face showed no pain, only cold contempt. He watched the flesh blacken. After a few seconds, he pulled his hand away. He examined the charred ruin of his palm. Then he looked at Lugosi. "Fiction?" he repeated. He flexed his fingers. The burned skin began to heal, slowly, visibly. "You made me look weak. Mortals must fear me, not laugh. Not think they know how to end me. Dracula fears nothing!"

Lugosi's mind fractured. Reason dissolved. Instinct took over. Survival. He remembered the role. His props. He always carried things. Tokens. He fumbled in his coat pocket. His hand closed on cold metal. He yanked it out. A small silver crucifix. A film prop. He thrust it towards Dracula. "Back! Get back!" His voice was a shriek.

Dracula looked at the cross. He laughed, a short, hollow sound, like stones cracking. "Props," he said. He snatched the cross from Lugosi's trembling hand. He held it tight. Silver burned his flesh again, smoke rose. He ignored it. He crushed the cross in his fist. The metal bent, twisted. He opened his hand. The mangled lump of silver fell to the alley floor with a dull clink.

Lugosi whimpered, he scrambled backwards. His hand hit something leaning against the wall. A wooden handle. A stagehand's broom, broken. A splintered piece of wood jutted from the end, like a stake. He grabbed it, held it like a spear. He pointed it at Dracula's chest. "Stay away!"

Dracula sighed. A sound of infinite weariness and contempt. He stepped forward, ignored the pointed wood. Lugosi lunged, desperate. He drove the splintered end towards Dracula's heart.

Dracula's hand moved. Faster than sight. He caught the wooden shaft an inch from his chest. He looked at Lugosi, held his gaze. Then he squeezed.

The wood didn't just break, it exploded. It shattered into useless splinters in Lugosi's hand. Shards stung his face.

Lugosi screamed. It was raw terror. He turned, ran. In blind panic he bolted down the alley, away from the impossible thing, the real monster.

Dracula let him run. He watched him go. A predator assessing his fleeing prey. He gave Lugosi ten seconds. Ten seconds of desperate, gasping flight. The alley opened onto a dimly lit side street. Lugosi stumbled out. He looked around wildly for help. The street was empty.

Dracula was there. Standing in front of him. He was blocking the way. He hadn't run, he'd simply appeared.

Lugosi screamed again. He turned and ran the other way. Down another alley. It was narrower, darker, a dead end. He skidded to a halt at a brick wall. He whirled around.

Dracula stood at the alley entrance. He was silhouetted against the weak street light. He walked forward, slow and deliberate. Each step echoed in the confined space. He wasn't rushing, he was savoring the terror. He was demonstrating the reality Lugosi had only pretended to know.

Lugosi pressed his back against the cold bricks. There was no escape. He slid down the wall, cowering in fear. "Please...please...I didn't know...I didn't mean..."

"You meant fame," Dracula stated. He stopped a few feet away. He was looming over Lugosi. "You meant profit. You used my shadow. You made it small. Manageable." He leaned down, close. His eyes burned into Lugosi's soul. "You invited the world to challenge me. That can not stand."

He reached down, fast. His hand closed on Lugosi's shoulder. He lifted him up. Then, slammed him back against the wall. Lugosi cried out. Pain shot through him.

Dracula's other hand gripped his jaw. It forced his head back, exposed his throat. Lugosi thrashed, kicked, punched. His blows hit Dracula like he was punching stone, useless.

Dracula bent his head. His lips drew back. His fangs glinted in the dim light. They were long, sharp and deadly white in the gloom. They were definitely not stage props, they were real.

Lugosi's scream died in a gurgle as the fangs pierced his flesh. It was deep and cold. Fire spread from the wound, not pain, a terrible, draining cold. It was life rushing out. He felt it. A river of warmth pulled from his veins. His struggles weakened, became feeble twitches.

Dracula drank, deeply and hungrily. Weeks of starvation focused on this one source. This vessel of insult. He drained the life, the vitality, the stolen fame. He took it all. Not just blood but also essence and years.

He stopped before the end, before death. He pulled back. Let Lugosi slump to the filthy alley floor. He wasn't dead, not quite.

Dracula looked down at him. Lugosi was a wreck. His skin was corpse-pale, wrinkled and sagging. His hair was stark white, thin. His eyes were sunken, clouded. Tremors wracked his frail body. He looked ancient. He was drained and hollow. He tried to speak, only a dry rasp came out.

Dracula knelt beside him. He studied the ruin he'd made. A cruel satisfaction caused a smile to appear across his lips. His smile shimmered then faded away. He leaned in close. His whisper was like ice in Lugosi's ear. "Now, *you* look like me."

Lugosi's eyes widened. A horrified understanding dawned on him. He saw his own withered hand. He felt the terrible emptiness inside, the weakness, the unnatural cold. He tried to scream again, nothing came.

Dracula stood. He looked at the broken shell of a Lugosi in front of him. Killing him would be a mercy. It would also end the story. It would raise questions. There would be investigations. The world believed Béla Lugosi was Dracula. The image, however flawed, spread his legend. It created fear, recognition. It was a tool.

A cold calculation formed. He needed the face. The public identity. The fear Lugosi generated could be harnessed. It could be controlled, made real.

He stripped Lugosi. The fine clothes came off his frail, shivering body. Dracula removed his own formal attire. He dressed Lugosi in his clothes. They hung loose on the shriveled frame. He pulled the stage Dracula cape from Lugosi's discarded costume. He wrapped the broken man in it, a shroud.

Then Dracula dressed himself in Lugosi's clothes. The suit from the premiere. The shirt, the tie. He smoothed the fabric. He ran a hand through his own dark hair, sweeping it back. He adopted the posture. The tilt of the head. The proud bearing Lugosi used on stage. He looked down at the real Lugosi, bundled in the cape on the ground.

The lines blurred. The impersonator lay broken. The real monster wore his skin.

Dracula walked to the alley entrance. He paused, looked back once. Lugosi's terrified, ancient eyes stared back. A living warning, a testament to the true horror. He was unable to speak, unable to move. He was barely alive.

Dracula turned away. He stepped out onto the Hollywood street. He walked with Lugosi's confident stride. He held his head high. He hailed a taxi. It stopped.

The driver looked back. "Where to, Mr. Lugosi?"

Dracula smiled. A slow, deliberate crooked smile formed on his face. Lugosi's famous smile, but colder, hungrier. "Home," he said, his voice a perfect mimic of the actor's cadence. "Drive."

The taxi pulled away. Dracula settled back in the seat. He watched the bright, false lights of Hollywood stream past the window. He was here. The legend walked among them. Now, it walked on his terms. The fear would remain. It would grow. It would be real.

In the dark alley, wrapped in a monster's cape, Béla Lugosi trembled. He listened to the fading sound of the taxi. The city's pulse buzzed around him. A pulse he could no longer feel in his own still veins. His eyes, wide with eternal horror, stared into the nothingness. The final reel had run. The credits would never roll.

About the Author

Laughton J. Collins, Jr. was born in the 20th century but currently lives in the 21st century. He is originally from Georgia—currently living somewhere in the Pacific Northwest—in and/or around the Seattle area— His work has been published in resurrection magazine issue II: crucify, March 31, 2024.

Also by Laughton J. Collins, Jr.

1. ghost riders in the sky and other lines (2023)
2. J^M!3– Anthology: Volume I (2024)
3. Shadows & Light: Haiku/Senryū (2024)
4. ghost riders in the sky and other lines (deluxe edition) (2024)
5. Paper View (2025)
6. The God Who Breaks: Old Testament Plays of Rebellion and Despair (2025)

My Website

THE HORROR OF IT ALL

STORIES

THE
MIDNIGHT PALACE

CRAWLER COVE	CURSE OF SHADOW PEOPLE	FLESH HARVEST

CRAWLER COVE

CURSE OF THE MIDNICHT PALACE

FLESH HARVEST

LAUGHTON J. COLLINS, JR.

THE HORROR OF IT ALL

STORIES

THE
MIDNIGHT PALACE

CRAWLER COVE	CURSE OF SHADOW PEOPLE	FLESH HARVEST

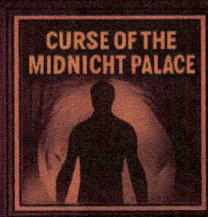

LAUGHTON J. COLLINS, JR.

THE HORROR OF IT ALL

STORIES

THE
MIDNIGHT PALACE

CRAWLER COVE	CURSE OF SHADOW PEOPLE	FLESH HARVEST

CRAWLER COVE

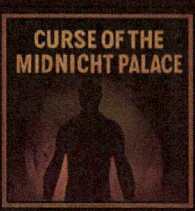

CURSE OF THE MIDNICHT PALACE

FLESH HARVEST

LAUGHTON J. COLLINS, JR.

THE HORROR
OF IT ALL
STORIES

THE
MIDNIGHT PALACE

CRAWLER COVE	CURSE OF SHADOW PEOPLE	FLESH HARVEST

CRAWLER COVE

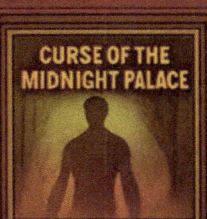
CURSE OF THE MIDNIGHT PALACE

FLESH HARVEST

LAUGHTON J. COLLINS, JR.

My Website

Social Media

Link Tree

Bookshop

Facebook

Authors Den

dot.profile

Amazon Author Page

ghost riders in the sky and other lines sample

Poem Hunter

Bluesky

Bookwire

My Website

Social Media

Link Tree

dot.profile

Facebook

Authors Den

Goodreads

Amazon Author Page

ghost riders in the sky and other lines sample

@LAUGHTONJCOLLINSJR

E-Mail

Books2Read

Goodreads

Bookshop

Books2Read

Substack

@LAUGHTONJCOLLINSJR

Shadows & Light on Amazon

www.ingramcontent.com/pod-product-compliance
Lightning Source LLC
Chambersburg PA
CBHW071218260626
47162CB00004B/1341